JOAN

Forgotten Women of History Book 1

ANNE R BAILEY

Copyright © 2017 by Anne R Bailey

All rights reserved.

No part of this book may be reproduced in any form or by any electronic or mechanical means, including information storage and retrieval systems, without written permission from the author, except for the use of brief quotations in a book review.

For my family

We loved with a love that was more than love.

— EDGAR ALLAN POE

ALSO BY ANNE R BAILEY

Forgotten Women of History

Joan

Fortuna's Queen

Royal Court Series

The Lady Carey

Other

The Stars Above

You can also follow the author at: www.annerbailey.com

PROLOGUE

Joan de Geneville's hand shook as she began her letter with the last of the precious ink she'd been allotted.

Where was her strength?

Trapped in this drafty house for the crime of being married to the wrong man, she was left with a pittance of an allowance for her keeping.

A particularly cold gust of wind hit the house. It crept through unfixed cracks in the wall, causing the temperature in the room to drop.

There was no fire to protect her.

Joan calculated if she could hold out for a few more weeks she would have enough to pay for a fire each day when winter truly arrived. In her whole life, she had never had to worry about things like this. Now fires were an extravagance; after all, Joan could barely afford to keep herself fed, not to mention her servants.

It was November 22, 1330, and news had reached her that her husband, who was imprisoned in the Tower of London, had been sentenced to death.

Earlier she had been cursing the man she had loved. The man who was to blame for her current imprisonment.

Now she desired nothing more than to see him one last time. As that would be impossible, she would commit her thoughts to paper.

How the wheel of fate turned.

Just months ago he was ruling England as de facto king. Now her husband would be hanged and she would likely die in her prison.

If not for the greed of men and the weak hearts of women, she would not be here.

Joan prayed that her letter would reach him in time. That he would be allowed to read it. She wished her strong-willed grandmother and stern mother were still here guiding her steps.

The two women had been instrumental figures in her life, even as a child when she was too young to understand.

It was nearly dark by the time she finished writing. Joan did not bother sealing it, knowing it would be read before being sent anyway. With a smile, she handed it to her maid and lay back in her straw bed. She shivered, but this time it was more out of fear than from the cold.

All Joan could think of now was the hangman's noose and if she would be subjected to it.

She could picture how her mother would scoff at her weakness. "You must be strong in the face of adversity," she would scold.

For all the love between them, Joan always seemed to fall short in her mother's eyes.

But then again, Joan de Geneville had always been a disappointment.

Born in the winter of 1285, at Ludlow Castle in England, she was not the heir her father desired. Nor did her mother find any joy in her arrival. Jeanne already had two daughters from a previous marriage, so the birth of another was simply unremarkable.

Her father, Peter de Geneville, never treated her cruelly, though. He could find no fault with her. She appeared to be a healthy, handsome babe with bright green eyes and a ready smile. He delighted in her charms and took to referring to her as his little doll.

When Joan was two years old, she was joined in the nursery by another sister, Maud. Beatrice followed a year later.

After the latest addition to his brood, her father, having lost interest in her mother, began increasing his travels to Ireland, the seat of his family's power. He finally took permanent residence with his father, the Baron Geneville, lord judicator of Ireland.

By then Joan was old enough to notice his absenteeism and wept miserably to be allowed to go with him whenever he left. At first she blamed her mother for separating them. However, she knew that the true blame lay with her father.

Her father continued to sully Joan's opinion of him when she heard her maids gossiping about how he had taken up with the daughter of a minor lord in Ireland. At the time, Joan had not known what this meant, but she assumed he had done something bad. Especially from the way the maids were discussing it.

Three years passed. Joan continued to reside with her mother and sisters at Ludlow. Her mother managed his estates with an efficiency that surprised many and allowed her husband to enjoy his freedom in Ireland. She lived as a single woman with the power of a married one, and it suited her just fine.

However, peace never lasted long in their family, and on a late summer day a messenger galloped up to the main gatehouse.

He carried news that would change Joan's life forever.

CHAPTER 1

1292

"Your father is dead." The words were spoken with a firm voice and carried a finality about them that left the six-year-old Joan gaping at her mother.

The little girl felt her eyes well up with tears and she trembled, trying to keep them at bay. Her mother seemed to approve of this and softened for a moment.

"He loved you very much. But now there is important work to be done. Your grandfather will arrive within the week to make the necessary arrangements for the funeral. This affects you most of all as your father's sole heir."

The child blinked in confusion.

"You will inherit everything that is not set aside for your sisters. Does that not please you?"

Joan nodded, even though she still did not quite grasp the importance of the situation.

"Nurse, take Lady Joan to her room and see that she gets a good night's rest."

Nurse Milly, who was standing off to the side, rushed forward and led the little child away.

Alone once more, Jeanne paced the length of the solar. Her

mind was churning with all that had to be done. Arrangements would have to be made. Joan stood to become one of the wealthiest heiresses in England. If Jeanne had her way, with her daughter's good breeding and wealth, an excellent alliance could be formed.

As her mother, Jeanne would also benefit, as she could now live independently and in the lap of luxury, provided that Joan's grandfather allowed her to retain wardship over her own daughter.

She bit her lip at the thought.

The old man was always kindhearted, and with their good relationship she did not see how he could refuse her this request. After all, she had managed the family estates now for nearly five years on her own and proved to be quite successful at it.

Still, Jeanne could not help but worry over her own future. At the age of forty-one, she only had her illustrious family name to recommend her. No one would want a dried-up old spinster. But after a life of disappointment at the hands of men, she looked forward to the prospect of independence.

Meanwhile, in her rooms, Joan, as the elder sister, gathered her siblings around her and told them the news. Neither of them had any recollection of their father, so they did not feel the pang of loss that Joan did.

They were also too young to understand the gravity of death.

Regardless, Joan, acting as their leader, commanded that they should be very sad and that tomorrow they would pick flowers for their father. Beatrice, who could barely walk, gurgled happily.

The nursemaids watching them shook their heads at their childish innocence, but it was not their place to comment. They also watched Joan with particular sadness and jealousy. She would be inheriting riches beyond their dreams, but she would also be fought over by hungry suitors. No doubt Joan would be pushed into an early marriage.

Within the week Baron de Geneville arrived with his retinue at Ludlow.

The house had already gone into mourning and a dour mood had settled over the place. Despite this, there was an efficient harmony to the household that de Geneville appreciated. His daughter-in-law proved to have a good head on her shoulders.

He was greeted in the great hall by a blazing fire. Lady Jeanne stood to greet him, her ladies and three daughters trailing behind her.

"Welcome, Father." She curtsied low.

He kissed her cheeks in familial affection. "I am sorry to see you in such sad times. But to be honest, my son had little more than wool between his ears, and so it is no great loss to our house."

Jeanne did not reply but gave him a soft smile.

"And these young ladies must be my granddaughters." He peered at the trio, studying them. He lingered on the eldest, Joan, with her green eyes. She seemed small for her age, dressed in a formal black gown and cap, but she looked promising enough.

A small nudge from their mother reminded the two oldest girls to curtsy, albeit clumsily, to their grandfather and introduce themselves.

"You must be hungry after your long journey. I have arranged for a light meal of pheasant and sweetmeats to be prepared in your honor."

"Gracious as ever. My men will eat here in the great hall, but I hope you will do me the honor of dining with me in private, as we have much to discuss."

Jeanne nodded.

They retreated to the solar, accompanied by a footman and a maidservant to wait upon them.

As they walked, Sir Geoffrey de Geneville noted the improvements made to Ludlow. It had been almost a decade since he had last stepped inside the house, and he was pleasantly surprised by what he saw. It had clearly been maintained well and tastefully decorated without being overly extravagant.

There were new tapestries hanging on the walls and a sweet scent of lavender seemed to linger in the air.

Sometimes he wondered at that son of his, who had proved to be such a disappointment. Peter had squandered his wealth and position. He spent his life pursuing pleasure rather than taking up any responsibility or showing any sort of ambition—a sin in Geoffrey's eyes.

There was no one to blame but his mother, who had spoiled him as a child. Even in adulthood, she had rewarded his laziness by bestowing upon him all of her English holdings.

Having finally reached the solar, he claimed the seat nearest to the fire.

At the age of sixty-six, he was finally starting to show his age. Most of his fellow peers had long since passed away, while until recently he had still been going strong.

The pair ate in silence for several moments. Both trying to determine the measure of the other.

"Would you like some more wine?" Jeanne inquired, breaking the silence.

"No. I have whetted my appetite enough. I feel both of us are ready to speak of more important matters." He took a moment to collect his thoughts. "My son's death came at an untimely moment. He left us without a proper heir. Even his eldest daughter is barely six—she is healthy, isn't she?"

JOAN

"Yes, she was always the picture of health." Jeanne reassured him.

Her father-in-law nodded his approval and continued. "At least there will be time to groom her properly and arrange an appropriate betrothal for her." He stroked his gray beard, thinking of potential families.

"And what of her wardship?"

Geoffrey felt the tension rise in the room. It was uncommon for the mother to retain custody of her children after the death of the father, but he was too old to think of rearing children and had his own business to attend to in Ireland. He could trust no other to keep the family fortunes and lands intact.

"I spoke with my lady-wife Matilda on the matter." He paused again. "We think you ought to retain custody of the children. Of course, changes will have to be made. Matilda feels Joan should have a tutor for Latin and history. As our heir it is important she is somewhat educated, as unconventional as it may be."

"Thank you, sir." Jeanne took his hands in hers and kissed them in gratitude.

"There are other arrangements to be made for the other girls."

"Sir?"

"They should enter the nunnery. That way they will not be able to contest any claim on Joan's land in the future."

"I assure you I would not let them." The thought of resigning her younger daughters to a nunnery did not appeal to her.

"I do not doubt your daughters, but their future husbands. Men are greedy by nature. I will not be swayed in this matter." He stood firm.

"Of course, milord." Jeanne acquiesced, hiding her disappointment by focusing on the happier news.

"I ride for London in a fortnight. When I return I hope to have made the arrangements in regards to Joan's future." He stood, wiping his hands on a napkin. "Your hospitality has been happily received, but now I am afraid I must retire for the night. My old bones cannot handle traveling as well as they used to. We shall speak more in the days to come."

Jeanne thanked him once more and bid him good night.

Before she retired, she went to see her children.

She crept into their room, as they were fast asleep already.

They looked so angelic. She placed a hand on Joan's head, stroking her soft dark hair. There would be so much pressure put on her. And her sisters would no doubt in their jealousy grow to hate her. But for now they were still children and could enjoy each other's company.

In an uncharacteristic show of motherly affection, Jeanne leaned over each of them and kissed their brows.

CHAPTER 2

1296

Joan ran through the bailey, chasing after Maud.

"Come back here!" she hollered.

"You have to catch me." Maud laughed, running even faster.

Even though she was only eight years old to her older sister's ten, she was much quicker on her feet. It also helped that she wasn't wearing the heavy skirts of an older child.

The duo continued their games well into the afternoon. They ended up side by side, leaning against each other on a bench. These gardens were their favorite place in the whole world, lying among the flowers and staring up at the sky.

"Maud?"

"Yes?"

"What are you looking for?"

"I'm trying to see the fairies. Cook says they live in the garden and make everything grow, even babies. She says this is where Mother found us."

Joan giggled. Babies grew inside women—everyone knew that—but she did not correct her younger sister.

"I heard fairies are bad and snatch up curious children to

take them to the fey lands, where they keep them there forever."

"No!"

"Yes!" Joan laughed and began tickling her sister mercilessly.

The girls were interrupted by the tiny figure of their youngest sister.

"Mother is looking for you." Her voice was quiet.

Unlike her older sisters, Beatrice was a sickly soft-spoken girl who even at such a young age was already a recluse.

"Fine." Joan sighed, getting up and trying to straighten her dress as best she could. Her mother always disapproved of unruly behavior. "Let's go, Maud." She held her hand out for her sister.

"Mother only wants you, Joan," Beatrice clarified.

"Oh." Joan shrugged. "All right. I will come find you later then."

"That sounds good." Maud grinned in return and watched her sister disappear. "What would you like to do, Beatrice?"

Beatrice played with the wooden rosary beads that hung from her neck. "We could play dolls, I guess."

While her younger sisters returned to their rooms to play, Joan was receiving a lecture.

"Why must you always run away from your nursemaid? And I do not want you running around with your sister as if you were peasant children."

"I am sorry." Joan looked down at the ground in an effort to avoid her mother's stern glare.

It had been four years since her father's death, and her mother still donned the traditional black cap and widow's weeds. It made her appear even older than her forty-four years and her taut face did nothing to help.

On the other hand, her serious manner ensured everyone took her seriously.

Jeanne pinched her nose in exasperation before continuing.

"I've received news from your grandfather. He has finalized the agreement for a betrothal for you. He has chosen Roger Mortimer, the eldest son of the Baron Mortimer. The ceremony will take place in August."

Joan gasped. She was to be betrothed!

Jeanne chuckled at her daughter's earnestness. She only hoped she would not be disappointed in the future.

"Will Maud be betrothed too?"

"No, not yet." Her mother did not want to tell her of the plans for her other sisters. "In the meantime, your grandmother will be arriving to attend the event, and I want you on your best behavior. That means no more running wild. You may work on your embroidery, or play with your sisters indoors. If you wish to go outside, have a maid accompany you. You are growing up and soon it will be time to put childish things behind you."

Joan nodded, her expression growing grave. "I promise I will do better, Mother."

"Good. See that you do. Now run along."

At first, Maud was ecstatic for her sister, but it did not take long for jealousy to overcome her.

Joan, who was always empathetic, realized this and reassured her that she would also get betrothed eventually.

Maud was unsure. As she braided her blonde hair that night, she made a promise to herself to become the best. She would show her mother that she could be just as successful as Joan, if not more so. Then her mother would arrange an even better match for her.

After that night the relationship between the two sisters shifted. It was barely noticeable. They still played, laughed, and cried together. However, a competitiveness that had not been there before developed. Each was trying to outdo the other.

Only Beatrice escaped this. Quiet as she was, her older sisters doted on her.

The sun grew hot and the days longer. Spring was giving way to summer, and the household found itself in an uproar.

"Why don't I get a new dress as well?" Maud complained, her voice getting louder by the second.

"Ouch." In her distraction, the seamstress had pricked Joan while altering her dress.

"Maud, if you cannot comport yourself as befits someone of your station, I shall forbid you from attending the betrothal ceremony." Their mother was having none of her disobedience.

Jeanne turned her attentions back to the seamstress's assistant. "Do you have any blue velvet swatches to show me?"

The assistant pulled a few samples to show her. "Either of these would suit the young mistress quite beautifully, milady."

Jeanne studied each carefully before settling on one. "This will do." The eggshell-blue cloth was an elegant but sturdy fabric.

Joan, who had been obediently standing still during her altering and measurement, turned her head around to see what her mother had chosen.

"Turn 'round, little lady," the seamstress instructed her.

Jeanne sighed. Perhaps it was her nerves about the upcoming months, but no one seemed to be comporting themselves the way they should be. She was running out of time, and there was still so much to plan.

"Joan, if you cannot behave, you will not be getting a dress either."

"I just moved a bit!" Joan defended herself but quickly shut her mouth under the hard stare of her mother. She spotted Maud pouting in the corner, looking angry with each second she was ignored.

It wasn't long before Joan saw Maud flee the room. She wanted to run after her.

Once again she felt guilty for the attention she was receiving.

Finally, making some excuse that she needed to go use the privy, she managed to slip out of her mother's grasp. She turned to go to Maud's room but heard a noise coming from her own.

Carefully, she pried the door open and peeked inside. There was Maud rifling through her things.

Joan watched as she pulled a burgundy gown out and tried to see how it would fit.

She did not mind that her sister seemed intent on stealing her clothes. If it made her feel better, Joan would have gladly given her more. She didn't want her sister to be mad at her—Joan never liked it whenever anyone was mad at her.

A few days later their mother demanded their presence.

They knew it couldn't be good, for they were hardly ever called into her private office where she conducted her business and heard petitions.

As they entered, Joan's eyes flew from her mother's stony face to the familiar red cloth in her hand.

Even from here Joan could tell the dress had been altered. The work was crudely done and the edges were frayed.

She realized Maud must have tried to alter it herself. She stole a glance at her sister and saw that she had gone pale.

Their mother began her tirade until finally Joan stepped forward and declared she had done it.

"I thought I might give it to Maud," she explained.

The look of fury she turned on her made Joan quake.

"What would possess you to do this? Hopefully, this can be salvaged, but what a waste of material." Jeanne seethed, pulling at the uneven seams. "You will receive ten strokes over your hands with the rod and no dinner tonight."

"Maud, if I can fix this dress, you may wear it. Nurse, please take care of Joan." Jeanne left the room.

Joan accepted her punishment with maturity and tried not to cry out. The nurse, who had her own suspicions about who the real culprit was, tried not to be too harsh.

Joan did not regret covering for her sister, who had undoubtedly done the deed. She watched as tears trailed down Maud's face. It was clear she felt regret too.

After the nurse left, Maud held Joan's hands in hers.

"I am so sorry," she sobbed.

"It does not matter. I would have given you the dress if you wanted it. I am sorry you aren't getting a new one of your own."

Maud wiped her eyes with the back of her hand. "No, I am so stupid! Who needs a silly dress? Can we still be friends?"

Joan nodded. "Of course, silly."

Maud hugged her tightly.

A peace settled over the household once more.

Maud tried harder than ever to ignore her jealousy.

In the middle of July a peculiar woman appeared in their lives. Matilda de Geneville was loud, brash, and still had remnants of dark red hair beneath her wimple. Everyone was taken aback by her wild attitude, but Joan loved her and refused to leave her side.

This was her grandmother on her father's side, and she told the most wonderful stories.

Where other adults preferred to ignore children, her grandmother even joined in their games—when no one was about, of course.

Joan would later learn that she was named after Matilda's daughter and her aunt. She had passed away after childbirth a year before Joan had been born.

"Your aunt Joan took after me," her grandmother would say as she combed and braided Joan's hair. "She had such bright red hair. It's a pity you did not inherit it."

Joan agreed. Her own plain black hair was nothing spectacular.

Time passed quickly for the four women in Ludlow. Even though Matilda tended to be a domineering woman, she was also astute and she let her daughter-in law Jeanne hold the reins. This was Jeanne's household, not hers, so she was careful to make only small suggestions here and there. In the end, she avoided stepping on any toes, or if she did, she did so politely.

Thus they lived harmoniously, and Jeanne was grateful for Matilda's influence on the children.

Joan, who was the most attached to her, had started to emulate her in every way.

She adopted her slow walk, head held high, as well as her calm demeanor. She sat beside her for hours doing needlework and hearing her stories. Many were very educational—stories about a year the harvest failed and how they dealt with it, stories about maids who stole, men who tried to swindle her, and how she fought with the king and privy councillor to ensure she retained her rights. Matilda had a gift for telling stories and always made them seem more exciting than they actually were.

During this time, the three sisters grew apart once more. Joan was being prepared for marriage, whereas her younger sisters were still in the throes of childhood.

Then Ludlow was overtaken by a new barrage of visitors. The visitors were the Mortimer family. Among the party was her betrothed. The young pair were kept separate from each other as custom dictated, but Joan was more concerned about the new aunts, cousins, and mothers that surrounded her. They studied her and exclaimed how surprised they were to find that she had become such a mature lady.

They fed her sweetmeats and braided her hair. It was a wonderful time, although extremely stressful for her mother, who was overseeing everything.

While they were fussing over her, her grandmother was haggling with Lord Mortimer over the marriage contract.

"I am ensuring your fortune shall be safe." Matilda was stroking her hair as she explained. "You bring a lot to this marriage. Don't you ever forget it."

"I won't," Joan assured her.

The day of the ceremony arrived sooner than Joan could have anticipated. Dressed in her new dress, she was directed to kneel on a pillow before the priest. The mass was dragging on and curiosity overcame her. She stole a glance at her betrothed, Roger. He was already tall, if not a bit scrawny, with curly light brown hair on his head.

The priest coughed and Joan quickly turned her gaze back to him.

There was an exchange of rings and suddenly it was done.

Feasting and dancing followed. The couple danced two dances, stumbling over the steps as the adults laughed and talked. Then they were ignored for the most part. Matilda held everyone's attention. She was clearly the matriarch here, and everyone was gravitating toward her.

By the time the Mortimers left, Joan had seen Roger, her fiancé, all of three times.

CHAPTER 3

1296-1297

Ludlow fell quiet as the festivities surrounding the betrothal of the young heiress dissipated.

Joan was not aware of her own importance, but her mother sure was.

The question of who she was to marry had occupied her grandfather for many months. Several families had been approached. The significance of the wealth and land she was to own was nothing to balk at, and King Edward I had to approve the marriage. He was not about to create a dangerous faction in his kingdom.

Jeanne wetted her dry lips as she stared at the crude map of England laid out before her.

After her marriage, her daughter would control the north of Ireland and much of the north of England.

Her father-in-law had told her that the king's own nephew had inquired after her hand in marriage. The king had been furious and rejected the idea immediately. That ambitious little traitor. It was no secret he coveted the crown, but he was powerless except for his blood relation to the king.

After her betrothal, Joan was no longer allowed to dine with her sisters in their nursery.

She did not mind this and found that being allowed into the world of adulthood was intriguing. Joan was also quickly learning the importance of rank and power. No one ever ignored her requests, and the servants always gave her their full curtsies. This was something that had previously only been reserved for her mother.

While she was still only eleven years old, she realized she had become someone very important.

She pondered this as she ate her food in the nimble fashion she had been taught. Her nurse, who still dogged her steps, had looked approvingly at her table manners.

Opposite of her sat her new tutor, Master Banner. He was an old man and constantly in a foul mood. He drummed Latin into her head with a ferocity that frightened her at times. Joan preferred learning arithmetic to languages. Luckily, she was already fluent in French and only had one other language to conquer before he would be satisfied.

Once when she had asked him why he looked so disappointed to be here, Master Banner had looked flabbergasted at her forwardness then proceeded to say he was here at the request of her illustrious grandfather and that he saw it as an insult to him that he had to teach a mere girl.

"I studied in the courts of Italy." He had wagged his finger in her face as if that was supposed to mean anything to her. "Now I am in this dreary place with a stubborn, ungrateful student."

Joan's reply had been swift and showed the quickness of her mind. "You are right, I am a mere girl. But it was my grandfather that decided you are only good enough to teach one and nothing more. I wonder what he would say if he hears you are ungrateful or that you believe he was mistaken in his assessment of your skills." Joan paused wickedly, letting her threats sink in. "I think I shall write him a letter about this matter. In Latin."

Master Banner had been silenced forever after that.

In his monthly report to her mother, he had stated that Joan showed promise as a conniving courtier and predicted her husband would have a hard time reeling her in.

Jeanne had taken the report with a smile and knew that her daughter was developing quite a powerful personality; she would not be a sheep.

In this world of men, this may not have been seen as desirable, but Joan was different. She could afford the luxuries of standing shoulder to shoulder with men, for she would be more powerful than half of them.

After that, an uneasy truce had developed between master and pupil. This time it was the pupil who held the power, because instead of punishing Joan for her outspokenness, Jeanne had encouraged it. Jeanne meant to teach Joan about ruling through Master Banner. The poor old man was at his wits end dealing with two domineering women.

But he was at least glad that Joan was intelligent enough to value his wisdom and deferred to his teachings. She accomplished every task he had set out for her and applied herself with a renewed ambition to conquer Latin.

Jeanne stood and with a clap of her hands ordered the dinner away.

They were a small crowd tonight, just the immediate family, chaplain, and schoolmaster.

Joan made ready to leave and was wiping her hands on a napkin when her mother beckoned her to come over to her.

"Lady Mother." Joan bobbed in a small curtsy.

"I wish to speak to you privately. You shall come to my private rooms, after you have said your prayers for the night."

"Yes, Mother." Joan dutifully went to do as she was bid.

Her mother was the most domineering person in her life, and as her chaplain preached at mass every day, she had to obey and honor her.

Dressed in her nightgown with a simple robe wrapped around herself, Joan padded toward her mother's rooms, followed by a new lady's maid.

Joan loved her mother's rooms, although she was rarely allowed inside. They were decorated with tapestries she had brought over from France, and the deep colors entranced Joan with their beauty.

As she stepped inside, Joan waited for her mother to appear and began studying the scenes they depicted.

Jeanne caught her daughter gliding her fingers over one of them.

"Your half-sister sent that over to me."

"Really?" Joan knew that she used to have other sisters from her mother's previous marriage, but they were both dead now. It was just two years ago that Isabelle, the youngest, had died in childbirth. Her mother had been stricken at the news, despite the fact they had been estranged for several years.

"Yes, Mathe could do wonders with a bit of thread." Jeanne cleared her throat, forcing back the memories of France. "I wanted to show you something." Jeanne led her daughter away from the tapestries and to her desk.

"It's England," Joan exclaimed, noticing the map.

"Yes, and this is Ireland." Jeanne pulled out another sheaf of papers. "Your grandpapa lives here. These are his lands." She pointed them out.

"Oh." Joan was not sure how she should respond. Jeanne turned her attention back to England. "Can you find where Ludlow is?"

Joan focused, studying the coastline. From memory, she finally found the spot and was rewarded with a pat on her head. "This is Castle Wigmore, your fiancé's future inheritance, and the land in between, who owns that land?"

Joan shrugged at her mother's question. What did she care?

"It shall one day be yours. All of it between you and your husband." Jeanne realized that Joan was probably still too young to understand the magnitude of this. "Whatever happens, this will always be yours by right," Jeanne pressed with finality.

"But don't I give my troth to my husband?" Joan was confused. That was what she had been taught, and what she had sworn at her betrothal ceremony.

"In most cases this would be true, but you are a very special case." Jeanne tapped her daughter's nose. "Your grandfather and grandmother have stipulated in their wills that only you and your children will inherit and have claim over their lands. Your husband can manage them and draw an income from them but nothing more. Roger Mortimer comes from a great family, but yours is greater. So he was promised Castle Wigmore as his inheritance and in case of, God forbid, his death, you and your children shall inherit it too."

Joan's eyes were wide. "Truly? All of this for me?"

Jeanne nodded. She was amused at the wonderment on her young daughter's face. No doubt she was thinking of all the pretty things she could buy with this money, but there was a more pressing lesson she was trying to impart on her daughter.

"It is all for you, but you will always face opposition." Jeanne turned serious now.

"But if it is supposed to be mine, then no one can take it away." Joan crossed her arms in front of her chest.

"When you and your sisters share a cake, don't all of you fight for the biggest piece?"

"Yes."

"Well, the same can be said for the lords and ladies of England. Everyone will want to get a piece of your fortune. Your grandmother had to fight with the king for the rights to her lands. They will always try to find a reason to take them away from you, especially since you are a girl, but you must never let them. They are yours."

"I promise, Mama," Joan responded in solemn French. "I will fight the king if I have to."

Jeanne laughed, breaking the tension. "Fight him only with the law, nothing more. Now off to bed." And with a peck on her cheek she sent her daughter off.

She would have to continue instructing her daughter about the careful maneuvering of court and politics, but there would be plenty of time for that.

Joan's lessons continued on and on. Her head was filled with lessons on etiquette, music, and languages.

One morning when Master Banner was feeling unwell, Joan had some time to herself.

She decided to see what her sisters were doing and found them playing in their room with dolls.

Maud looked up as her sister entered the room and whispered to Beatrice, who giggled.

Joan knew she must have said something about her and frowned. "What did you say?"

"Nothing." Maud turned away and returned her attention to playing with Beatrice.

"Beatrice?" Joan inquired of her youngest sister. They had always been good friends, but now her sister refused to meet her gaze.

"Go away, Joan. Don't you have some grown-up work to do? Or studies?" Maud mocked.

Joan wanted to cry. Somehow she had been ostracized by her own sisters. But it was the betrayal of sweet Beatrice that stung her the most. Instead, she did as she was bid and returned to her own rooms where she would continue with practicing translating Latin.

In a couple of years Joan would realize that her sisters had suffered while she had been exalted. They were not important and were simply seen as spares. Their mother spared them little attention and the servants left them to their own devices.

The distance between the sisters had not gone unnoticed. Their mother studied the way they avoided each other's gaze, and while Joan looked calm and collected as she had been taught, it was clear that it was weighing heavily on her mind.

Jeanne wrote a lengthy letter to her father-in-law stating that perhaps it was time for her younger daughters to enter the nunnery. She had made inquiries and Aconbury Priory, just a full day's ride away from Ludlow, was willing to take them in.

In the weeks that passed Jeanne sat down personally with Joan, outlining how parliament and the legal system worked in England. She did not go in depth, for she did not know too much herself, but rather focused on inheritance laws and what would affect her daughter most of all.

Joan noted quickly how the odds were stacked against her.

She knew her grandfather had a younger son who had been disinherited due to his betrayal and involvement in the Welsh wars. He had not been executed because he was young and because of the position of her grandfather. Of course, there was nothing stopping him from declaring that he should inherit his parents' lands and fortunes once they passed away. He was still a male heir and who knew the way parliament would vote in a few years.

Joan learned in those few weeks how fickle parliament could be, and it was drummed into her head that she would have to be tight-fisted with everything she owned.

It had been nearly three weeks since her mother had sent the letter to Ireland. Joan, who had been walking in the garden with her maid, was the first to take note of a man in her grandfather's livery riding up the stone pathway to Ludlow.

Gathering her skirts about her, she rushed to her mother's side. She earned a stare of displeasure from her mother, but she was not sent away as her mother received the messenger.

"Milady." He bowed low. "I have news from my master." He held out a letter that he had pulled from a satchel by his side. "He is well and hopes that you and yours are well."

"Thank you." Jeanne took the letter but did not break the seal yet. "I shall send for some venison from the kitchen. My steward will see you are found rooms to rest." She nodded toward the man standing behind her.

The messenger bowed again and retreated.

Joan followed after her mother as she retreated back to her room to read the important letter.

"What is this about, Mama?"

Jeanne put a hand on her daughter's head. She was still short for her age and looked slight. "Nothing to worry yourself about, my dear. It is just news from your grandfather about the future."

"Is it about me?"

Jeanne frowned at her daughter's impertinent question. "Do not be so self-centered," she warned, as if noticing her daughter's behavior for the first time.

Breaking the seal carefully, she read the letter out loud.

Matilda wished to see Joan and asked for her to be sent to her in Ireland for a few weeks, as soon as possible. Geoffrey had approved of her sending the younger girls to Aconbury Priory. He would send generous donations for their dowries in order for them to be able to become brides of Christ.

"What does he mean? Are Maud and Beatrice to be sent

JOAN

away?" Joan was confused.

"Yes, for the betterment of the family they shall be sent to learn and become nuns. Every great family sends some of their children into the church to pray for our sins."

"But..."

Jeanne knew the excuse was unsubstantial, but she did not wish to explain to her young daughter that it was the request of her grandfather that had led to this decision. Many families sent away their children, not only to pray for the family's eternal souls but also to ensure and protect the inheritance of others. Besides, at least her youngest daughters would be spared the pain of childbirth and the trials of marriage.

"Enough. You shall be packed up and sent to Ireland. Focus on your own good fortune." Jeanne sent her away with a wave of her hand.

Curtsying, Joan fled her mother's rooms. She did not go tell her sisters. She was perhaps still too proud to break the silence between them, so instead she went to find Master Banner. With him she practiced arithmetic problems and it helped occupy her mind.

When she had finally calmed her mind enough, she walked around the garden. Her maid followed a few paces behind, no doubt wondering what this little lady was so pensive about.

Meanwhile, Joan was thinking of Ireland. She yearned to see her grandmother again—the woman had been a wonderful companion last time she had visited—but she was also old enough to know that she would likely never see her sisters again, or at least not for a long time. She was also nervous to be leaving her home for the very first time.

She wished to force herself to be happy. Everyone expected her to be so—all the time.

Joan bit the inside of her cheek, a nervous habit she had developed. She noticed the way they mocked her sometimes.

The servants and tutors—she was but a small little girl playing at being an adult. Her mother dressed her in fine clothing and had her walk around filled with self-importance, but all the while they remembered how mere years ago she was a babe and still was in many respects.

Having gotten her fill of walking around the castle grounds, Joan turned on her heel and headed back to her rooms.

Her maid was the daughter of one of the many tenants on the land. She was a simple thing who was hardly a proper companion to her, but for ten-year-old Joan she would do.

Joan could never trust her to understand instructions, nor would she ever confide in her. She knew her mother had become friends with her ladies-in-waiting, but she could never see herself befriending Mattie.

Two days later, Maud and Beatrice were called before their mother. They were not used to being summoned in this formal way and came in holding each other's hands. What had they done wrong?

Jeanne smiled down at her nervous daughters as she set aside her accounts book and bid the steward step forward.

"I am pleased to see how well you girls have grown up. I have heard both of you are quite polite and behave according to your station. Thus it pleases me to tell you that your grandfather has deemed that you two shall enter the Aconbury abbey and begin training as nuns." Jeanne beamed at her daughters as her little speech came to a close.

Maud was agape. She did not know much about being a nun but knew that they did not get married. They lived like priests in the churches. She scrunched up her nose at the thought of living and working in an abbey. She found mass dull and could not stomach the thought of never being able to leave.

"But why, Lady Mother? What have we done?" She finally

spoke, her voice a low whine.

Jeanne's displeasure showed immediately. "It is a great honor to be able to serve your family and be called to serve God in this way. You will be given a great education and lead a holy life. I will not hear another complaint from either of you."

Maud bowed her head in shame, but inside she was still fuming with childish rage at the unfairness of her lot in life.

When she and Beatrice were sent to their rooms once more, she left her younger sister and stormed off to find their older sister.

Joan was pacing the great hall, reciting poetry she had to memorize for Master Banner, when she spotted her sister.

She wanted to run when confronted with her fierce gaze but instead squared her shoulders and prepared herself for a fight.

Hands on her hips, Maud approached. "What did you tell Mother?"

"Nothing." Joan was honest about that.

"I suppose you will be happy to learn that you will have Roger all to yourself and be the only one of us to be married, even though I am much prettier than you." Maud spoke venomously.

"What is that supposed to mean? Roger is my fiancé. Of course he is mine." Joan clutched at her book of poems.

Maud smirked. "Well, I met and talked to him a few times. He told me I was pretty and gave me a flower. I bet he never called you pretty."

Joan scrunched her brows together. Truth be told, she had barely talked to her fiancé at all. She had never been left alone with him either, but she did not let her younger sister win. She held up her left hand.

"You see this ring?" The gold ring seemed to flicker in the sunlight that poured into the room. "Roger gave it to me. I am to be his wife, not you. So keep your flower; it means nothing. This ring means everything."

Maud took a step back, for she had been outdone. She had expected her sister to be jealous, just as she was. She had wanted to hurt her, just as she had felt when their mother told her she was to be sent away. Tears welled in her eyes and she fled the great hall.

The servants, who had stopped their work to stare, quickly pretended to not have noticed.

Joan calmed her breathing and, proud to have maintained a cool head, returned to her memorization as if nothing had happened.

Master Banner heard of this event and regarded the little girl he was teaching with a newfound respect. Perhaps he should teach her some politics and debate as well; she seemed to have a mind for it. Not that it would do for a woman to be so educated.

Within the next few days, many preparations were underway.

Jeanne would arrange a great mass and feast for her younger daughters who were to go to the abbey. She would travel with them to see them settled and pay their dowries. Then she would see Joan off to Ireland. For the first time in years she would be alone without children surrounding her. It suddenly made her realize how old she was to have another set of children grown up already.

Merchants were visiting Ludlow daily now. It seemed the castle had become in constant need of supplies and had developed its own little economy. Wheat and cheese, foreign wine, and cloth all the way from Italy streamed in. They had become a very popular and powerful family.

There was news from France as well. King Philippe was in talks with King Edward I to arrange a marriage between their children.

Jeanne wondered what plans the French king had for England.

She knew that England was suffering after being at war with Scotland for so long. Her own treasury was drying up paying for the taxes the crown kept demanding. It had been years of thrift that had left her with sufficient funds, but now between her daughters getting married or entering the nunnery and taxes, money seemed to be flowing out of Ludlow instead of into it.

With a sigh, she hoped that they would be able to manage praying for peace and an end to taxes.

Dressed in a bright blue gown and her hair braided with white flowers, Joan sat beside her mother as she watched her younger sisters receive Mass and holy blessings from their priest.

The two girls knelt before him on soft cushions, looking pious with their hair free and curled around their faces.

Only Joan knew of the anger Maud must be feeling, but like any good daughter she had been resigned to it. Beatrice was another matter altogether. She did not mind the thought of going into a nunnery. Joan suspected she would enjoy it, for she knew how her sister loved animals and playing in the garden. She would find it peaceful.

With the choir finishing the last hymn, the girls rose, dressed in heavy black dresses, as if they had already taken their orders and a procession followed after them.

The feast that night was grand. A suckling pig was served and all sorts of mincemeat pies and other treats as well. Their mother had taken care to serve their favorite dishes to honor her daughters. After dinner, the minstrel played lively tunes and the girls danced for the household as their mother clapped in time. As night fell a traveling troubadour recited his poetry and told them the epic tale of King Arthur and the Black Knight.

His voice was clear and strong. He turned Joan's thoughts away from leaving her home to pleasanter thoughts of courtly love and chivalry.

Finally, when everyone was exhausted, Jeanne called for the night to end and everyone began retiring back to their rooms.

The servants streamed in with dark bags under their eyes to begin tidying the great hall. They would work late into the night, and then they would have to be up before anyone else. It was tiring work.

The following day was clear and the sun shone brightly overhead. It was a good day to travel. Jeanne was overseeing the litter and wagon being loaded up. The hired guards that would accompany her and the two girls were already armed and mounted, waiting anxiously to set out.

The chest of gold containing three hundred gold pieces was carefully tucked away. It was a huge dowry for the abbey but would ensure that Maud and Beatrice be treated with the utmost respect for the rest of their lives and receive plenty of luxuries not afforded to other nuns. Perhaps one day if they applied themselves, they could become abbesses. Trunks carrying clothing were also stacked on top. They would be provided with everything except for their underclothes. So Jeanne ensured they had enough to last them a year or two.

With everything packed away, she bid the girls say goodbye to one another. Maud and Joan were cold to one another, but Beatrice flung her arms around Joan and hugged her tight.

"Take care of the castle," Jeanne ordered Joan, who nodded solemnly.

Of course, the castle was not under her watch while her mother was gone. The steward had taken that responsibility, but Joan would be the lady of the house while she was gone and sit at the high seat in the great hall at dinner.

JOAN

With a heavy heart, Joan watched as her mother rode off with her sisters. The wagons followed behind their litter at a leisurely pace. Her mother would return in a mere four days, but it seemed an eternity to the young girl. Turning away, Joan said a small prayer under her breath that they would all be safe and retreated back inside the familiar walls of Ludlow.

This was practice, she told herself, despite the overwhelming sense of loneliness. She held the keys of the house and was in charge. Even though she was frequently in her room alone either studying or working on her embroidery, she now felt the room altogether too quiet, and Mattie, her maid, was not much for conversation. Picking up her needle and thread, she retreated to the great hall and sat by the fire working as the servants went about their daily tasks.

She was working on fine embroidery that she would take once she was married. She had started working on a box of things since her betrothal ceremony. Her mother had decided that her skills were finally good enough and told her that she needed to apply herself to creating actual shirts and linen, not just practicing.

Joan did not particularly enjoy this task, but neither did she complain, as she knew that every great wife was good at all things and she would strive to be perfect.

That night at dinner, Joan called for the minstrels to play throughout the night, and she watched the more important servants dance and make merry. It filled the house with cheer and distracted her from her loneliness.

Master Banner approached Joan the next day with a new lesson—geography. She stared at the map of the whole of Europe with an intense gaze. Up until now she had only seen a map of England. She had heard of places like France and Rome but had not seen them laid out like this.

"England looks awfully small," she commented.

"Yes, but she is powerful."

Joan was curious how England could be a powerful player when it was so tiny a country, but she saved the question for another day.

"Here is the seat of the Pope." Master Banner pointed to the grand cathedral drawn on the lower half of Italy.

"That is so far away," Joan exclaimed, judging the distance. "How does he keep such power from so far away?"

"Ah! That is a very good question. One that I shall have you answer."

Joan bit the inside of her cheek, thinking hard on this. "It is our love and respect for the Christian faith that bends us to the will of the Pope, no matter how far away he is. Threat of excommunication and the desire to be holy in the eyes of God. That is how he holds power."

Master Banner nodded his agreement. "Very well thought out. Think that in all of Christendom, if the Pope decides to excommunicate a king or disagrees with policies, then he can call upon all of Europe to rise to his cause. The Pope holds both physical and psychological power over all of Christianity. As God rules over us all."

Joan crossed herself. She marveled at the Pope's power but knew it was precarious as well, for if all the rulers of the realm decided to not follow him or fell into heresy, then the Pope would be just another bishop. That was another lesson her mother had taught her many times. Power was given by those you rule, and while it was true that it was her right to rule and have possession of these lands, she needed the assent of the people to keep it.

She would need to keep the people in her domain happy, lest they rebel or grow to despise her and try to put someone else in her place.

The rest of the night was spent memorizing the locations on the map. Of course, it was unlikely she would ever step foot outside of England, but it was still important for her to know where everyone was and where the wool she produced was sold and how far it traveled.

Joan went to bed with a feeling of her own insignificance in the face of the world laid out before her. She had never felt this before and it humbled her.

Rising early the next day, she led the house to prayers and listened to the family chaplain and the small choir singing hymns and blessings over the congregation.

∽

Time passed faster than she could have realized. Between overseeing work in the household and trying to play the lady, soon it was the fourth day and a runner announced that her mother approached.

She awaited her mother with a feast. She knew the party would be hungry after traveling all day, and she thought this would be a nice gesture to show her mother how responsible she had become.

Her mother entered, and Joan knelt for her blessing and greeted her mother with a kiss on her cheek.

"Will you have some refreshment?"

Jeanne smiled at her serious daughter. "Yes, sit with me, little woman."

The pair sat side by side with the rest of the guards and servants that had accompanied her taking seats around the head table and grabbing what food they could off the platters.

Jeanne poured herself some wine and took a few gulps. "Maud was quite a handful. I did not know she had gotten so spirited. The church will do her some good." Joan could only imagine, but she didn't press her mother for what Maud had done.

"How was the journey? Was the priory nice?"

"We had good weather, praise be to God. The priory was

well situated and managed. The nuns there are kind, and your sisters will be well taken care of."

Joan let out a sigh of relief. That was good to hear. She felt guilt over her lot in life, but she also envied her sisters their assured lives. If her studies had shown her anything, nothing would be certain for her on the path that lay ahead. She dreamed of a peaceful future where she would live calmly with her husband at Ludlow surrounded by their children.

But England was at war even now and had always at some point or another been at war. Life was about fighting, and while she could dream of peace she knew it was unlikely she would see much of it.

These dark thoughts lulled her to sleep that night, strengthening her resolve to survive.

Her mother was occupied with other thoughts. With her two daughters tucked away in the priory, she now had to send Joan off to Ireland. It was for the best, she thought, for she had heard that the fighting was encroaching farther south. Rebellions and fear were spreading through the countryside like wildfire. Perhaps it would truly be best if Joan were sent off to the relative safety of Ireland for the time being.

~

A ship was hired to carry her, and a handmaid, two scullery maids, and four guardsmen were selected to accompany her. Jeanne wished she too could make the journey, but she had too much to oversee here. The king had written to all his vassals urging them to stifle any rebellion in their individual lands and to round up more volunteers for his wars. Sometimes Jeanne wished to complain about the hardships her husband had left her with, but she was confident in her own strength and refused to bruise her pride by admitting any weakness.

The first day at sea was tough on Joan. Her stomach

churned as each wave rocked their small merchant ship.

On the second day, Joan seemed to finally get her sea legs and was comfortable walking around the deck of the ship. Her handmaid was struggling to keep up with her mistress. Standing at the bow of the ship, Joan watched as land came into view and soon the port emerged.

She was excited but couldn't hide her nerves. This was a strange land and she was alone.

It took a while for the ship to reach the harbor and longer still for her to finally disembark. On shore was a retinue of servants from her grandparents' household. They bowed low to the girl who would one day be their mistress.

A man stepped forward and she recognized him as the man who had attended her betrothal ceremony with her grandmother.

"My lady, you are welcome to Ireland." He swept another courtly bow. "I have come to escort you to your grandmother and grandfather."

"Thank you." Joan acknowledged him with a bow of her head.

She climbed into a waiting carriage and her maid climbed in after. She was not concerned for her things. The servants would take care of them.

Instead, Joan occupied her time by staring out the window as the litter pulled by no fewer than six horses rushed through the countryside.

There was a wild beauty to this land she had not seen in England. The grass appeared to be a deep emerald green and the sky was bright blue overhead.

She noticed the tall spires of the churches before she saw the rest of the city. Here was Dublin, the center of all of Ireland. Joan knew from tales that Ireland was considered to be unkempt and barbaric compared to England, but as they stopped for a fresh set of horses she did not see anything of the sort. The women and men were dressed in a different fashion and they seemed to follow fewer conventions, even walking around with their hair uncovered, but there was nothing uncomely about them.

By nightfall the manservant tapped the carriage door to inform her that they were arriving at Trim Castle.

Sure enough, when she looked out the left side of the carriage she saw the tall bailey and the castle walls coming into view. Among the flat plains it was an imposing figure on the landscape. As the sun dipped behind the horizon, it illuminated the castle in a soft glowing light. Like one out of her fairy tales, or so she imagined.

As she was helped out of the carriage, her grandmother, dressed in a regal dress of forest green and white, came running down the steps of the castle. Her steps were spry, like a woman half her age.

"My darling," she exclaimed, throwing her arms around her precious granddaughter.

"Grand-mère." Joan returned the familiar hug.

"How was the journey? Are you cold? Hungry?" Matilda laughed, leading her inside. "Come, I shall fatten you up and you shall grow tall."

Joan chuckled at her grandmother's antics. She had never been so familiar when she was at Ludlow.

In the great hall, her grandfather sat by the fire wrapped in furs and surrounded by his servants.

He stood and accepted Joan's greeting with a soft smile. "You are growing into a fine young woman. Almost ready to be married, eh?" He grinned when he saw her blush of embarrassment.

"Come now. This is no place for blushing ladies. Ireland is a land of tough lords and ladies who would skin you alive."

Joan gasped, but all around her grandfather the servants

and visiting lords laughed at his joke.

"You have nothing to fear from these good people," Matilda said, putting a hand on her granddaughter's shoulders. "You will get used to their sense of humor. I am afraid Lord Geoffrey here has taught them quite badly."

Once more Joan was led away to a table where plates of hot boar and greens were placed in front of her. She watched from afar as her grandfather spoke to the barons around him, listening to their complaints and getting advice from others.

He was working as the king's representative and was the go-between of the great lords of Ireland. It was a tough job, but somehow Geoffrey had found a way to placate both parties and he had kept his position longer than any other person.

Matilda sat across from her with a ready smile. "Forgive our informal greeting and behaviors. You will find we are easy-going but just as clever and quick to insult as our English cousins."

Joan gave a nod before she scooped more food into her mouth. She was hungry and had craved a warm meal.

"How are things in England? How are your mother and sisters?"

"They are well. Beatrice and Maud have been sent to the abbey. They did not want to go, but Mother said they had to for the family."

"Will you miss them?"

Joan thought for a moment but could only shrug. In truth, she was unsure if she would miss them. It felt as if it had been years since she had been close to them, but perhaps she would.

"Mother is well. She was loath to see me depart." Joan grinned.

"All mothers hate to see their children grow into adulthood." Matilda patted Joan's arm, assuring her. "You will see when you have children of your own." She paused for a while. "That husband of yours. Do you like him?"

"I don't know him," Joan answered honestly.

"Hmm." Matilda thought for a while, turning her gaze to her busy husband. "Well, we shall have to make sure he is a good husband who will take care of his lands and his people. Just like your grandfather has. In the meantime, I shall introduce you and teach you to love this place."

Joan wondered what she could learn in such a short time, but she wasn't about to disagree with her beloved grandmother.

"Have you finished your meal? I'll have your maidservant take you to your rooms and I'll take care of your guards and see that they are fed."

Joan thanked her, stifling a yawn.

There wasn't much to do in the next days besides sit with her grandmother as she pored over the histories of Ireland. Which clan was fighting with which and who were all the important people of the land. Joan wondered why she could not have just stayed in England for this, but she did not voice her opinions.

The next week, her grandfather urged her to come on her first hunting expedition. She knew it was a popular pastime, but her mother had never held one on their lands.

"Are you secure in the saddle?" her grandmother asked as she helped her up onto the gray mare.

"Yes." Joan shifted slightly to get comfortable.

"Ride well and hold on tight," Matilda whispered and said something in Gaelic. For luck, she had said.

The party took off with the barking of the hounds at their heels. It was a lot of hard riding through the forest before they picked up the scent of something.

The men rushed forward to give chase to the deer. Her grandfather, still spry as a young man, arched his English bow and took aim. The first shot missed, but the second was true and felled the deer.

Joan gave up a cheer with the rest of the party, the adrenaline having caught up with her as well.

They returned home by nightfall, and the cook prepared the deer.

"Did you enjoy yourself?" Matilda came to sit beside her granddaughter.

"Oh yes." Joan beamed. "I hope we can go again. Why did you not come with us?"

Matilda chuckled. "Your grandfather is athletic enough for such an endeavor, but, alas, I have aged far beyond him and cannot keep up. I think I should like to take you to the Witch's Hill though. We can have a picnic there."

"Witch?" Joan's eyes were wide.

"They say the fae live there and that a witch used to dance and live on top of the hill in the cottage. Of course, it is just a tale the peasants tell, but in the early morning there is an eerie fog that covers the place. It looks quite haunting, to be sure."

"I would like to go," Joan murmured.

"And so we shall. Now let us retire and leave the men to their drinking and boasting. You shall have to show me some of the embroidery you do, and I shall show you the tapestries I have fashioned." Matilda led the little Joan away, for the men were getting increasingly rowdy. She did not know how her husband matched their level of energy, but she suspected it kept him young.

Before she knew it, the weeks had rolled by and soon it was time for Joan to depart and return to her mother. She had been taken to visit all the important local lords and had toured the countryside with her grandfather. Her grandmother had been an anomaly. She was a strong woman with her own opinions, and her husband had not turned her away, nor did he laugh at her. He respected her wisdom. Joan wished that her own marriage would be like this.

So it was with a heavy heart that she left the green and

wild Ireland. She had reconnected with a piece of her ancestry that she had never known before. She rode down the foothills her own father had ridden and explored the many great houses in which he had been raised.

~

Jeanne, who had been anxious for her daughter's return, was surprised to find a bonny little woman in her place.

"You stayed in the sun too much." She frowned, taking in her daughter's darkened complexion.

"We explored all of Ireland," Joan exaggerated, ignoring her mother's concerns.

"Yes, well it is better that you are home now. There is much work for you to be done, and you cannot fall behind in your studies."

"Of course not," Joan promised, although inside she loathed the thought of returning to studying Latin.

Jeanne would have laughed at her daughter's easygoing attitude, but she did not have the energy to. Things were turning serious, and several of the men she had sent to fight in King Edward's wars had died on the battlefield.

While Ireland may have been enjoying peace, the land here was in turmoil. It was still early days and there was no reason to worry her daughter just yet. Soon she would have to learn about warfare too and how to organize provisions for a siege, should it ever come to that. Jeanne crossed herself, praying to God it would never happen here in Ludlow. It was true that Ludlow was a wealthy land, but they had neither the strategic position nor fortifications that would attract the Scots to bring war to them. Or so she hoped.

She had heard from Maud frequently. Her daughter begged to come home. She enjoyed her studies (or so she claimed) but did not wish to take her orders. Jeanne sighed.

Her daughter would have to recognize the opportunity she had been given and bend to the will of the family.

She replied to her daughter with cool impassive remarks that she was to remain at the abbey and continue being a good pupil.

Jeanne had also heard from the abbess that her younger daughter Beatrice was proving to be a very bright pupil. The youngest girl diligently did all her chores and had an affinity for looking after the livestock on the premises. Jeanne was happy to hear that at least one of her daughters was settling down. Joan still had a ways to go, and once she was married then Jeanne herself could relax.

CHAPTER 4

1301

Joan could hardly believe where the time had gone.

Now she stood almost shoulder to shoulder with her mother.

She was no longer a child pretending to be an adult.

Her head stayed raised high as she walked, showing how unmistakably proud she had become. Her mother's chaplain constantly warned her against the sin of pride and vanity. She said her Hail Marys and tried to do penance, but she could not help the way she had been raised to feel.

Last month Joan had celebrated her sixteenth birthday, and her mother declared it was time that she was married. The wedding was being prepared with incredible attention to detail.

She would live with Roger after they were married at his father's home.

Joan could not think of leaving the familiar walls of Ludlow. She knew every corridor and room. She had grown up here and was loath to leave her home.

Her mother had been kind enough to arrange a household for her. She would not be going to her husband's home empty-handed. Joan called it her small court. It had been decided that Master Banner, a manservant, groomsmen, three ladies, and a chamberlain would be accompanying her. Master Banner would act as her steward and tutor all at the same time. As per her marriage agreement, her grandfather had transferred to her ownership of Ludlow and several smaller castles and their lands for her to manage and earn an income from.

Truthfully, in the five years that had passed, her grandfather had aged significantly and he no longer wished to travel to England. So he did not mind giving her and her husband some of her lands. Besides, this was only a quarter of what she stood to inherit, and Joan was very grateful for every penny.

Additionally, her mother had commissioned for her a new litter that was decorated with the coat of arms of the de Genevilles and the blue azure coat of arms of Roger Mortimer to signify their union. There were also several new dresses for Joan to enjoy. She was a wealthy heiress, and when she appeared before her husband he would see her value.

Joan was excited at the prospect of all of these new changes and the grand position she was being given. She felt like a princess.

༽

Before the wedding she was to visit her sisters at Aconbury Priory and from there travel to Pembridge Manor, where she and her mother would stay until the marriage.

Her new handmaid, Abigale, plaited her hair for the journey and pulled it into a bun. Her shining black hair had grown long and she had not wished to trim it. After her wedding, she would wear crespinettes to cover her hair, as was the style of a proper married woman. For now Joan still enjoyed the freedom of being a free woman. She enjoyed the admiring glances the boys and men on her lands gave her. The merchants who came to the castle to speak with her mother always tried to catch her attention, but she would not be swayed by their compliments.

Her mother had warned her not to be persuaded by pretty words and empty gifts. Joan touched the ring on her finger. This was the only gift with meaning. She'd known it when she was merely ten years old, and now it was engrained into her very being. Marriage was the only honorable gift and promise a man could make. Only her husband was worthy of her love and devotion. No other man should exist besides him and the Lord in her eyes.

While Joan believed and repeated this solemnly to her mother, she could not help but add that she hoped her husband would be worthy of her love. That he would treat her with the same respect and that he wasn't hideous nor would he be abusive. These hopes and prayers she kept to herself, lest she be seen as ungrateful.

Still, Joan did not think this would be a possibility. Things like that did not happen to people like her. Or so she had been led to believe due to her sheltered upbringing. Her mother prayed that her daughter would not have cause to see the world for what it was, but sometimes she regretted having raised her daughter to feel such invulnerability.

Joan had not been to court since she was a child, and here around Ludlow they were the wealthiest family. No doubt she thought herself the best in all the kingdom, with the prettiest fashions and the most opulent jewels. That was far from the truth, but Jeanne supposed her daughter would see the error of her ways eventually.

Ludlow was in an upheaval getting ready for the departure of their mistress. Lady Jeanne would return to tend the land in her daughter's absence, and in time Lady Joan would return to manage the estate herself. In the meantime, the servants of the castle were preparing to send their mistress off with all her belongings for her marriage.

Unlike the king's court, they were not used to packing up and moving from place to place on a whim of their master. So Jeanne and Joan had to carefully oversee the packing of all their belongings. An ox and cart were hired to take some of the heavier items that Joan would not need right away. She had convinced her mother to allow her to take her chests and drawers with her so she could have a piece of her family with her at all times.

Finally, on a warm spring day the party set out south for Aconbury Priory.

The countryside was quiet on their way there and Joan looked on happily, waving to all the villagers they passed.

When the party finally reached the abbey, it was late in the afternoon. Everyone was tired, but Joan was excited to be reunited with her sisters. She hoped she would have their forgiveness and that the time apart had healed wounds between them.

The abbess came out in her severe nun's dress and habit and greeted the two ladies with all the reverence they deserved. In turn, both Jeanne and Joan bowed deeply to the religious woman.

"Come, I am sure you are weary from your journey but wish to be reunited with your two youngest." She spoke in a soft voice to Jeanne, who nodded with a smile. "This way." The pair followed after her inside the grand abbey.

The smell of incense struck Joan and lulled her into a stupor. The air was fragrant with the smell of cloves and lavender. The high walls were gloriously decorated with lilacs on each pillar. At the front of the abbey was the chapel with the grand altarpiece. It had a huge gold cross and a stained-glass window behind it, created an imposing figure. Joan was taken aback and she had to cross herself at the sight of it.

They were led in the back to a hall where several nuns were working by the fires or singing hymns and saying prayers. Others were working on tapestries and embroidery while there was still some natural light left.

Two figures stood up and slowly walked toward them. These girls were young and clearly had not taken their vows yet. Joan recognized them immediately.

Beatrice still had the golden hair of her childhood while Maud had matured into a beauty that even the vain Joan could not deny. She swallowed hard and remembered how her fiancé had given Maud a flower. She was prettier than Joan was. Would Roger be disappointed?

Both girls curtsied to their mother and embraced Joan as sisters should. They were taken to a more secluded room where they could sit together and catch up.

Joan, for once, was in the background as her mother inquired how her daughters' studies were going.

Beatrice had a knack for working in the garden, even though it was not something ladies of her stature usually did. She helped tend to the sick and had embraced her life here with a passion that surprised even her mother.

Maud was different. It was clear she was not happy here, but she had learned better than to voice her opinions.

While Beatrice spoke kindly to Joan, Maud refused to look at her for long.

"Well, we shall retire. Tomorrow your sister shall cleanse and hold vigil with you girls. Then she shall be off to be married," Jeanne ordered, standing from her cushioned seat.

Joan found it hard to concentrate on her prayers the next day. While things had chilled between her and Beatrice, she couldn't help but feel as though they had drifted too far apart to ever fix the rift between them. Besides, they were for different worlds now. Joan would be married while her sisters would stay in the church for life.

JOAN

When the hymns came to a close and Joan was finally allowed to rise from her kneeling position, her legs were asleep and she struggled to rejoin her mother. Maud giggled at her and under her breath said she hobbled like an old lady. Joan would have retorted, but she felt like she should be the bigger person and did not say a single word but fixed her sister with a stare before stepping inside the waiting litter.

"What did you pray for?" her mother inquired as the carriage rolled away.

"For the success of my marriage," Joan responded. What she had said was half a lie, but her mother nodded, approving her response. Most of the time she had spent in holy reverence she had actually spent daydreaming. Hardly proper and something she could never admit to her mother.

"Your husband shall be your master now, and you shall have to follow him in all things. I know this may be hard for you at the beginning, for you have never had such a man in your life, but you must swear to obey him and you may find that you shall be partners in all that you do," her mother explained.

Joan would have laughed had she not seen her mother's serious expression. "I shall try to obey, but I feel that I would do a good job running everything myself. You have run Father's lands for years and even acted as my guardian."

"Yes, but not all men would think this is appropriate," Jeanne warned. "And I only did so because I had the permission of your father and grandfather. So show your husband you have a smart head on those shoulders and you shall see he will respect and trust you."

Feeling better, Joan nodded and turned back to staring out the window of the carriage.

At their current lumbering pace it would take two days to reach Pembridge Manor.

Joan was surprised to see how grand the house was. It matched Ludlow in many ways. Perhaps even surpassed it in some respects. She was even more surprised by all the armed men stationed around the house.

"They are off to war in the north," Jeanne said, reassuring her anxious daughter.

"Right."

The herald announced their arrival and the guards stood at attention as their carriage passed through the gates and into the heart of the manor.

A servant led them inside to where all the Mortimers were arranged to greet them.

The greetings were exceedingly formal and all decorum was observed.

"You and your daughter shall stay in the rooms by the chapel, and your servants too shall be given lodging. Tomorrow we shall hold the wedding feast for these young lovebirds, and then I am off to war," Lord Mortimer announced, placing a hand on his son's shoulder.

His hurried speech and jolly attitude put everyone at ease. He spoke of going off to war as if he was talking about taking a stroll through the gardens.

That was how Joan knew she would like him.

She also turned her attentions to her husband-to-be. He had grown tall. Before he had been the same height as her, but now he towered over her by at least a head. He had light brown curls littering his head, but his most impressive feature was his dark piercing eyes. Joan blushed when he caught her looking at him and quickly looked away. For her part, she hoped he was as pleased with her as she was with him.

Regardless, they would not be left alone until after the wedding feast tomorrow. She and her mother were led away

JOAN

by the women in his family. Her new mother-in-law had a pinched smile and small beady eyes. Joan hoped they would be able to get along, but she didn't place too much hope, for already the woman was scowling at everything she or her mother did.

They slept together in the same room. It was large and richly decorated. The fire kept the room toasty and they were served delicious sweet wine and meats.

"How do you find your home?" Jeanne asked her daughter as they sat around the fire together. This might well be the last time they would do this for a while.

"I like it." Joan's voice was uncharacteristically quiet. "It seems like a grand place."

"Your husband is handsome. I am sure you two will get along quite well. You must remember to be on your best behavior and act like a proper lady. Maybe one day soon you will go to court as well." Jeanne brightened at the thought of court. She had only been there once, at the coronation of King Edward I. She had only been a young girl herself, but the opulence of court had taken her breath away.

With a heavy sigh, Jeanne turned to the bed waiting for them. "We should retire early tonight. Tomorrow is a busy day and you should be rested."

With a nod, Joan clambered under the covers. Soon mother and daughter fell asleep.

The next day Jeanne shook her daughter awake. It was just before dawn. She had instructed the maid to wake her. She would help her daughter get ready for her wedding day and make sure she looked spectacular.

Joan was less excited at the prospect of her marriage now, and her nerves were taking over.

"Where is the brave young lady that I know?" Jeanne chided as she ran a comb through her daughter's long hair over and over again until it shone in the light.

Joan looked down, embarrassed that her mother realized what she was feeling. She steeled herself to be happy today. She did not want her husband to see her crying like a babe for her home or for missing her mother.

"Abigale, please fetch her dress. It must be time for the ceremony." The maid scampered off to fetch the gown.

Now alone, Jeanne thought it might be practical to give her daughter some advice on her wedding night. "Tonight, just remember to relax and do what your husband commands. Since you are married, it is a godly act and it is your duty as his wife to satisfy him. It can be a pleasant experience, and I do not believe your husband will be cruel."

Joan shuddered at the thought, but her mother's words helped her relax. It was her duty to become Roger's wife, and it must be what God wanted of her as well. She spared a smile to her mother, who squeezed her hand reassuringly.

After she had bathed and dressed in a new soft cream-colored petticoat, her wedding gown was placed over her head. It was a rich yellow silk gown. A string of pearls was laid at her neck, and a gold circlet fixated a white veil over her head.

She looked like a princess and felt like one too.

Her mother led her out of the room, where Roger's mother and sisters waited to follow after her.

She walked down the aisle to greet Roger, who gleefully took her hand in his. Guests on either side were seated as the priest began the ceremony.

The whole time Joan was breathless. She could not believe she was getting married, that tonight she would truly become a grown woman.

As she once again promised her troth to her husband and he lifted her veil to place a kiss on her lips, she lost the fright she had felt this morning. Instead, she gave him a coy smile and they walked back down the aisle hand in hand to the applause of their families.

JOAN

They broke their fast at the head of the table and were treated with great honor. Musicians played throughout the breakfast.

"Are you pleased with me, my lord husband?" She grinned as he fed her a piece of succulent pheasant.

"Yes, quite. You have become quite beautiful, my dark wife." He returned her smile. "I am quite lucky." They raised their glasses to each other and drank deeply. "We shall have food and celebrations all day. There will be an archery competition and a hunt, followed by dinner and dancing well into the night," he informed her.

She nodded excitedly, for she loved a good celebration.

The rest of the time she spent accepting gifts from family and friends. They were given generously by each side of the family for the new couple to start their new life together.

Joan met Roger's sisters and younger brothers during this time as well. Roger had four younger brothers and three sisters. His oldest sister, Maud, was already married to a knight and had two children by him. They had been married only three years. She seemed quite friendly to Joan and was constantly at her side, telling her who was who and pointing out funny little stories about each of her new relatives.

Joan was happy to get to know her husband and his kinsmen. From her first impressions she was sure they were well suited for one another, but time would tell.

"How do you find the Marches?" Roger inquired, knowing she had ridden through them on the way to Pembridge Manor.

"They seem to be quite beautiful. It would be wonderful to explore them one day."

"You aren't afraid of ghosts?"

"Ghosts?" Joan repeated incredulously.

"Oh yes! There are rumors that at night you can hear the eerie screams of drowned victims. A Roman army had been swallowed up by the mud many years ago, you know."

Joan waved him away. "There is no such tale."

"How do you know? He practically pouted his lips.

"I learned that the Romans never made it so far north. Besides, the Marches don't look like they could swallow up anything." Joan defended her thinking.

Roger laughed. "I did not expect you would be so smart."

Joan smiled at him. "Wouldn't you be bored otherwise?"

Roger placed a kiss on her cheek. "Likely. I cannot stand my mother and sisters. All they do is talk about clothes and sing hymns."

"One day I shall take you to Witch's Hill in Ireland. There you will find real magic and ghosts."

Roger grinned at the prospect. He had been taught about Ireland and loved tales of chivalry. He imagined himself the rescuer and his wife the damsel in distress he would rescue. "Do you think I shall be named Lord Protector of Ireland?"

Joan frowned. That would mean displacing her grandfather. She loved him and he had always been kind to her. "Maybe, once I inherit."

"We inherit," Roger corrected her. For what was hers was now his as well by law.

Joan bit her cheek to keep from retorting and demanding to know what he was contributing to this marriage, but she knew better than that, especially when they were in public. So she decided to play the obedient wife and dazzled her husband with a smile.

"What are you two talking about?" Lord Mortimer came up to the pair. They seemed to be getting along already. Seeing how they quickly turned their eyes to their laps, he placed a hand on his rounded belly and laughed in pleasure. "Let us see the archery competition."

Outside on the castle grounds a makeshift stand and box had been set up.

Joan and Roger were seated at the forefront and given the

best seats in the house. Their parents sat behind them and the guests took their seats in the stands. Wine and ale were passed around by servants as the competitors bowed before the couple and presented themselves to the crowd.

With the blare of the horn the first round began.

Most shot true and hit their targets square on, but those that didn't were booed off the competition grounds.

Four more rounds passed, and as the targets moved farther and farther away only a few remained in the competition. They now shot one by one, and the crowd waited with bated breath to see if the target would be hit.

Finally, there seemed to be a winner. The last man standing was a handsome young fellow with dark hair and a scruffy beard. Before he could be declared the winner, Roger jumped to his feet, challenging the poor fellow to one more round.

"Get me my bow and arrow," Roger called as he raced to the yard. He was intent on impressing his new bride.

A servant came running.

Both men took their positions and aimed their arrows. With a wink to Joan, Roger let his arrow fly. It hit the target but not squarely in the middle.

His competitor took a deep breath and let his arrow loose as well. He hit the bull's-eye. The crowd cheered.

Roger looked deflated and he was angry but decided to be jovial and put his arm around the winner.

"Three cheers for our marksman here!" he shouted before returning to his wife's side.

Joan would have laughed at his boastful attitude but knew better than to make fun of a man when he was down. She placed her hand in his and whispered how she hadn't known she had married such an athletic man.

He grinned, suddenly happy once again, and rewarded her with another kiss. As it was their wedding day, it was appropriate for him to show so much affection and it led to more celebration, as it seemed the couple were so well disposed toward one another.

∼

It was late in the afternoon when horses were brought around for the family. They would go on a short hunt as dinner was prepared.

Jeanne watched as her daughter was helped to her horse by her husband. She chuckled to herself. She knew full well that her daughter did not need help getting on her horse, but wishing to please her husband, Joan let him help her. Jeanne would not be surprised if she managed to wrap her new husband around her finger by the end of the week.

The master of the horse gave a loud yell and the trumpets announced that the party was leaving.

Roger pushed his horse forward and matched pace with his father, who was on a black steed looking every bit the lord. Joan followed behind with her mother.

Roger's female relatives hung back. He had explained that his mother hated to ride and his sisters had never been taught.

"I'm glad you know how to ride," he told her. She had blushed at his suggestive tone.

The hounds were unable to find anything and the party returned back home, disappointed but still excited from the day's festivities.

A warm dinner and music were waiting for them. A couple of performers had also been hired and they put on a makeshift play about the Scots invading England and being thrown back into the sea. It was a comedy, but Joan realized that it was the truth of what King Edward was now trying to do. He wanted the Scottish crown for himself and was at war with the barbarians in the north. Joan shuddered to think that her own husband might be called to serve in the army. It surprised her that she was concerned about his safety already. It also dawned on her that they were now responsible for each other's well-being. As she cared and worried for his safety, he would worry for her as well.

She determined that in the morning she would pray that the fighting would end quickly.

The party gorged themselves on roast pig, stuffed quail, mincemeat pies, and sausages. There were also fruits and sweet cakes served by the platter. Joan had to stop herself from eating more. Already her dress felt tight, as if it might burst at the seams.

Beside her Roger was content drinking away and joking with his friends who were seated by him.

Later, as the food flooding out of the kitchens slowed, the musicians began playing with renewed vigor. It was dark now and the warm light from the fire and candles cast a warm glow about the great hall. A dance floor was opened up and couples led each other to the dance floor.

Joan looked at Roger with a coquettish grin plastered on her face.

Guessing what she wanted, he stood, holding out a hand for her to take. She accepted graciously and he led her to the others on the dance floor.

He danced well. His feet carried him gracefully through all the steps of the latest dances. Joan found it exhilarating. Dancing with a dance master had not been like this. It had never made her feel flushed or hot with both embarrassment and passion. The way he looked at her made her feel as though she was the most beautiful woman in the world.

With the end of the song, the hall clapped for the young couple who had danced so well for them.

Joan all but ran back to her seat to hide from all the eyes on her. She was still not used to the attention.

She saw her mother-in-law casting disapproving glances at her as if she was leading her son into temptation. As if they had not been married in the eyes of the church and God. Merely dancing together could not be seen as anything sinful.

Joan would have huffed and made a scene, but she knew that they were going to live together and it would be best to live in peace and harmony rather than fighting, so she ignored her feelings and smiled back at her.

Her mother walked to her side and placed a comforting hand on her shoulder as she looked about the room. These people were their new family through marriage. They looked like a lively bunch. One day soon, Joan and her new husband would be the head of this great family. Jeanne hoped that her daughter would be able to lead alongside her husband with a clear head and intelligence while also taking care of her own estates.

Jeanne knew her daughter was likely to face a lot of opposition and hardship in her life, but she hoped the excellent education she had provided her would see her through.

"I am pleased with your match. Your husband is quite handsome." She winked at Joan, who had returned to being the blushing bride.

"It's not for his handsomeness that I married him." Joan shrugged as if it did not matter to her.

"So an old man would have been just as nice? Would he have made you smile and laugh as much as your Roger has?" Jeanne teased. She was happy her daughter seemed so well matched with her husband.

"Mother, really." Joan restrained herself from swatting her mother's hand away.

"I am planning to leave tomorrow. I have to keep an eye on your estates now and safeguard your future until you can manage them yourself. You will write to me with any news," Jeanne pressed. It was not only news of her daughter's well-being that she was after, but she also wanted to know family news and gossip. "I heard you may be going to court. You will have to send me news."

"Of course, Mama. I shan't forget," Joan promised. She wanted to add that she would have preferred it if her mother would stay with her. It would help to have her support and guidance in this strange new place, but she supposed she would learn on her own.

Master Banner was approaching the high table. He was a hired servant, but as a tutor he held prestige and was present at the day's celebrations.

"I have a gift for you," he said, his voice gruff as he handed her a box wrapped in animal skins.

"Thank you." Joan stood over the table and gave him a quick kiss on the cheek. "You have been a great tutor even as I have been a most stubborn student. I hope you will continue serving me and guiding me as you have always done."

Banner gave a little bow and retreated.

When Joan pulled back the animal skins it was not a box she found but rather a small book. It must have been done by his own hand. She opened the cover and felt the soft vellum under her fingertips.

"*Roman de la Rose and Other Poems*, an appropriate gift." Jeanne read the title over her shoulder.

"What is it? I haven't heard this poem before." Joan flipped through the pages written in French and admired the illuminations that Master Banner must have had commissioned. The Ballad of King Horn was also included. It was not a long book, but it was touching he had gone through the effort. It must have cost him at least two years' worth of income, although he had not had any expenses while he had stayed with them these past five years.

"You shall see. It's quite romantic." Jeanne laughed. "You

must send him a purse of coins to thank him. It is only appropriate."

Joan nodded. She had many fine jewels and clothes now, but she had not had something as fine as this. A book of her own.

She would have to ask Roger if they had a library at Wigmore Castle. If not, she would start one. She swore she would be a great scholar and not let herself be an ignorant mule. She was an heiress in her own right and did not have to cleave to her husband's control as some women had to. Besides, Roger seemed to appreciate her wit and intelligent conversation.

The night progressed with more dancing and music. There was an ever-flowing stream of wine. Joan was getting quite tipsy. Her mother had returned to sit with their relatives and was going about the room making acquaintances of everyone.

Roger had returned to her side after fooling around with his friends. "I shall have to introduce you to my very good friend Simon."

"Of course, I would be pleased to make his acquaintance," Joan replied, searching him out in the crowd.

"Maybe tomorrow, my sweet." He leaned in, whispering in her ear if she would like to retire for the night.

A deep blush swept over her entire body. Joan wondered if she was hot to the touch, but she nodded to her husband.

Roger whispered to his groomsman and then after he left to go to his room said, "I shall see you in your rooms in a bit. Wilfrid will send your maid to you."

Joan remained mute and watched him disappear upstairs.

Sure enough, her maid soon appeared at her side. "I can take you to your room if you wish, my lady."

Joan stood and slipped out with her maid. There were cheers behind her as she left, which made her blush with embarrassment. It seemed that was what she was going to be doing constantly as a married woman.

Abigale led her upstairs. While her mistress had celebrated and dined, she had been hard at work memorizing the manor and getting to know how everything worked.

They climbed two flights of stairs until they reached the family quarters. This was the wing of the castle in which her mother-in-law and sisters lived. Her rooms were delegated to the very end of the hallway, the farthest possible from Roger's own room.

Joan frowned at that. Would they never have any privacy? For surely, any time she and Roger wished to be alone, his mother would know. She would bet this was his mother's doing. Trying to keep her son as far apart from his wife as possible. It was all right; Joan would ensure that this minor inconvenience would not separate her from her husband. She would be a good wife to him.

Abigale pushed open the heavy paneled door and revealed her rooms. There was a small private solar that Joan assumed could be used to conduct her writing and meetings as her mother did back at Ludlow, although this one was much smaller.

Beyond that, another door led to the bedroom. A wardrobe was set up for her, ready for the dresses she had brought with her. This would be moved to their primary residence at Wigmore Castle after the wedding.

The room was luxuriously decorated. Dried rose petals and herbs littered the floor, giving the room a sweet but not overpowering fragrance.

In the center of the room, there was a grand oak bed with intricately carved pillars featuring unicorns and angels.

The bed and wall were covered with both linens and tapestries Joan had brought and also with new ones from her new family.

Upon touching the mattress, she knew she had a soft feather mattress and from the looks of it plenty of warm, soft furs and quilts.

This was the bedroom of a woman and not like her childish room back at Ludlow.

Joan sighed contently. She could not complain about this room at all. A warm fire blazed as well.

Seeing her mistress was done exploring her new rooms, Abigale motioned for her to sit by the vanity where she proceeded to unclasp the crespinette from her hair and brushed out the tangles.

She brought a bottle of rose oil from a box and gently rubbed a bit of it into Joan's hair, simultaneously massaging her scalp. Then she brushed her hair again until it shone like black silk.

Finally, Abigale began undressing her mistress. The laces were loosened on her sleeves and carefully tucked away into waiting trunks. This dress was too rich to be worn every day and would have to be stored with the utmost of care.

Then the overcoat was slipped off. Joan was left in her soft cream petticoat.

"Do you wish for me to continue?" Abigale asked her mistress, who up until now was tight-lipped.

"No, you may go." Joan waved her away, dismissing her.

"I left a jug of wine and glasses for you. I shall sleep outside your room tonight if you need me, and I shall wake you in the morning for prayers." Abigale noticed how small and nervous Joan looked, but she said nothing. It was not her place. With that, she left the room and Joan was left alone.

Joan bit her lip nervously and wondered what to do now. She had nothing to do but wait, and it was not helping her anxiety. She could confidently take inventory of a harvest, she knew how much a household cost to manage, she could recite recipes for cheese making and brewing ale, but in the face of lying with her husband she was unsure.

A small knock at her door announced his arrival.

A manservant opened the door at her beckoning and Roger stepped in, dressed in a red robe and simple white slippers. The manservant laid down the tray of food he brought with him, bowed, and left the couple alone.

"Did we need more food?" Joan inquired, not knowing what else to say.

"Probably not." Roger grinned. "But I didn't know what else to bring."

"Well, as long as you do not turn yourself into a fat old man, I do not mind." Joan smiled back, then looked away from his gaze, blushing.

The couple was uneasy with each other, and at Joan's suggestion they took a seat by the fire. She poured wine for them into goblets, her hands trembling slightly as she handed the goblet to her husband.

"Shall we toast to something?" he asked.

"Our successful union," came the easy suggestion.

"As my lady wishes." He flattered her with a wink, made the toast, and they both drank deeply.

Silence once again filled the room.

"Tell me about yourself?" Joan once again was the first to speak out. He had been studying her with an intensity she found unnerving. "My mother told me you had trained as a squire under your uncle. Have you seen many battles?"

Roger seemed pleased with this line of questioning and began describing his time under the guardianship of his uncle in earnest. "At first..." He paused, as if shy about what he was about to admit, but she smiled and he continued. "At first, I was quite scared to be away from home. It was cold in the north and my servant had terrified me with tales of the barbaric Scots. I was sure they would climb through my window and murder me as I slept."

Roger gave a laugh at his boyish fear, and Joan laughed alongside him. She would not dare to make fun of her husband; she had been taught to have better manners than that. But she was quickly getting to understand the type of man her husband was: a fanciful, vain man.

"The training was hard. I am good with a sword, but I hated running about the castle on errands. That's also where I met Simon, who was the son of my uncle's blacksmith. We shared a room together and we learned to ride, hunt, and hawk together. He wants to become a great soldier one day."

"What about you? What do you aspire to be?" Joan inquired.

"A great lord, with the love of my people and..." He stood, taking her hand in his. "My wife. I shall make our family great and we shall prosper." His eyes seemed to shine in the firelight at his passionate speech, and it awakened Joan's own ambition.

"Together," she promised, adding her other hand on top of his. "We shall be great."

He kissed her hand then, and for once she did not blush under his gaze.

"You looked beautiful today. Like a true lady from one of the chivalric poems. I shall have them write poems and songs about you." His voice was a whisper as he continued to study her.

"Milord, I do believe you are trying to flirt with me. Take care, or else you shall make me become vain and I shall be forced to confess my sin tomorrow," she teased in reply.

"It would be a sin to lie."

He pulled her up from her seat.

Joan was flustered by his words. No man in her old household dared flirt with her like this. No visitor dared say such flattering things. Of course, her mother and maids had commented she was pretty, but it was not the same. So she found her heart pounding in her chest as she let her husband lead her to their bed.

They spent a large part of the remainder of the night talking about their respective childhoods. He asked about Ludlow and what Ireland was like. She asked if he had fought in any battles and what his siblings were like. That night they formed a tight bond between themselves. Joan was pleased with the respect and care he showed her.

She knew it was her duty to be more to him in time and hoped she would be able to give him an heir.

~

The next morning, the couple were still sleeping together when their respective servants entered the room.

Roger was grouchy at the rude awakening, but his groomsmen insisted that his mother demanded they attend church together and that he should get dressed, lest he anger her. Joan wondered at how quickly her husband went from man to boy. But the manservant was right: his mother and father still ruled here. They would have to respect their rules.

Giving Joan a quick peck on the lips, Roger left her rooms to return to his own. Only then did Joan call for her maid and get out of bed herself.

Wordlessly, Abigale prepared her mistress. As a married woman, Joan would now have to cover her hair. Another net and crespinette were chosen. This one made of silver thread decorated with white pearls.

Joan thoughtfully chose a deep blue gown with a white surcoat to complement the hairpiece.

As Joan was led to the family chapel, Abigale mentioned to her that she would have to pick out a few ladies-in-waiting to attend to her. As a married woman, she would have to gather a proper household around her now.

As the small choir began singing the hymns, Joan took her seat beside her mother and husband.

The priest had begun droning in Latin when Jeanne looked to her daughter and squeezed her hands. "Are you well?" she whispered.

Joan nodded in response. "Quite well, Mother." She threw a quick smile at Roger.

"I am glad. We shall talk after breakfast. I am to leave this afternoon."

With that, the women returned to listening piously to the priest.

After what felt like an especially long mass, the family filed out into the great hall for dinner, the other attendants following behind them.

Joan was seated across from her new mother-in-law and beside Roger's sisters. Her husband was three seats away, and she couldn't help but frown at that. Should they not be sitting together as husband and wife?

Her mother, sitting beside the lady of the house, nudged her with her foot under the table. Quickly catching her meaning, Joan plastered a small smile on her face instead. It would not do for her family to see the new bride frowning the day after her wedding.

"You shall join us for sewing today, Joan." Margaret, Roger's mother, spoke. It was not a question but a command.

"I am sure she would love to. She is quite capable with a needle and thread." Jeanne jumped in.

"Yes, I am sure she is." Margaret fixed Joan with a mean stare. This young woman had caught the attention of her husband and son with what she saw as haughty behavior and manners. She knew her daughter-in-law was an educated woman, who would no doubt make a wonderful courtier with her ability to ride and make merry. Joan de Geneville had not been her choice for her son. It had been her husband who had settled on the girl as the perfect match. Who was Margaret to disagree with him, especially when he had teased that she was simply intimidated by the girl?

Joan looked over to Roger, who was talking to his father and younger brothers. Would they not spend time together today?

"I would be pleased to help you select a few more appropriate headdresses," Margaret suggested happily.

Joan looked taken aback but schooled her features. "I would welcome your opinion. I do enjoy these crespinettes and the circlets and veil, but I surely need many more."

"Perhaps a coif and wimple would suit you too," Margaret, who was wearing a hideously plain wimple herself, suggested.

Joan smiled in reply and returned to her breakfast. She swore to herself that she would never wear such a thing. Already it seemed she had cast her mother-in-law as the villainess. Roger's sisters were equally boring and quiet. No doubt their mother had taught them how desirous they would be. Unfortunately, Maud, the one sister who seemed promising, had returned home last night. She had seemed to be the greatest potential friend Joan could make. She lived nearby in her husband's manor home with her young children. Perhaps Joan could visit her or have her visit at Wigmore Castle. Her mother Margaret could hardly disagree with such a choice companion.

Breakfast was carried away once everyone had their fill. Slowly, everyone went about their business. Lord Mortimer would be riding off in a mere two days and there was a lot to prepare. The rest of the household would be returning to Wigmore Castle as well.

Roger would be left in charge of the household, with his mother's guidance, of course.

Joan would learn that there was a lot to be done when a lord rode out to war. Supplies needed to be organized, and the logistics of resupplying them had to be established. Joan was surprised by the amount of armor and horses needed for such an endeavor. No wonder so many noblemen hated war. It was a costly affair, especially when there was little to be gained fighting the northern barbarians.

As promised, Joan sat primly with the women of her new family. She would have rather been helping her mother pack for her journey home, but she would obey her elders. She had started embroidering her initials and Roger's into a piece of cloth as a keepsake for her husband. Something simple that she could finish within a few hours.

The rest of the women were stitching shirts for Lord Mortimer to take on his campaign north.

Margaret was muttering under her breath. From the snippets Joan heard, she was saying prayers, as if she could stitch God's protection into the clothes. It was clear she was a pious woman, but Joan had to hide her smirk. She was not nearly that pious, judging from the grandness of her dresses. The bright colors and the rosary hanging from her neck that was embossed with diamonds and rubies showed a different side of her.

Joan would come to learn in later years that Margaret was a proud woman who tried to hide her faults behind her jewels and silks. As Margaret aged, she hid her disappearing beauty by playing at being pious. Over the following years, Joan would come to regret the discord that developed between them. Had she been a more intelligent young lady, she would have realized the ally she could have had in Margaret. That despite Margaret's lack of formal education, her life experiences and support would have been valuable to draw upon. As it stood, Joan quickly disliked Margaret, thinking her ugly and unkind. From the early hours, young Joan swore she would never be like the dour-looking Margaret.

"Girls, why don't you sing a hymn?" Margaret suggested to her younger daughters.

They quickly struck up in soft unison. Joan did not have this one memorized and could only listen as she continued to work.

After they finished, Margaret turned to her, asking if she could not sing.

"I am not as good as your own daughters." Joan flattered the two young girls. They smiled brightly at her. Elizabeth and little Jo were both destined for the church. With so many children, the family did not wish to split the family fortune into so many parts. Nor was it logical to provide so many dowries when a more appealing option was available. By entering the church, not only were the boys and girls provided with a stable and secure life, but they could even rise in the world, becoming leaders of the church or famous scholars.

The little girls, who were seven and five, respectively, had been caught in their mother's pious teachings and relished the opportunity to be able to take orders. In fact, they pitied their older sister, who had been married years earlier. So now they waited until their mother deemed them old enough to become novices at a nunnery.

Joan had been shocked when she heard how excitedly they talked of living in a nunnery.

All she could think of was her sister Maud's angry face when she had last seen her. She had heard her fighting with their mother for many days, crying and begging not to be sent away. She couldn't see why these two children were so excited but assumed that their mother had somehow tricked them.

Perhaps she was entering blasphemous territory, but Joan swore she would not subject her own children to the church.

Unless, of course, they had a calling for it. Then she would gladly send them.

She hoped Roger would be of a similar mindset.

Judging by how the sun crested overhead, noon had passed when Joan finally set her embroidery aside. She was nearly done and had even stitched a crude outline of Roger's emblem on the cloth.

"If I may be excused I would like to see how my mother is getting along. It must be nearing the time for her to depart."

Margaret looked at her for a moment as if wondering if she was lying. "Go ahead. Mary can take you to her," she said, nodding to a lady's maid behind her to take her.

Joan curtsied to her and departed, following after Mary.

With a careful nudge of the door, Joan entered her mother's room. It was the same room she had first stayed in when she had arrived. The room seemed small now compared to her own rooms upstairs. It hit her for a moment that there was no turning back now. This was her home. Her mother would leave. She would be alone.

Jeanne turned around from her luggage. She had been ordering Mattie to carefully fold her favorite gowns so they would not wrinkle on the ride home.

"There you are. How was your time with Lady Margaret?"

Joan looked at Mary, who was waiting in the corner for her to finish. "It was wonderful. I am glad to get to know my family so well. I have come to see you and how you are faring getting ready to depart."

"Well enough. I think we shall be on our way within the hour. I dare say, we shall have to stop at an inn on the way with the way I am finishing things here." Jeanne seemed exasperated; things had fit so perfectly together when they were at Ludlow.

Joan turned to Mary. "I shall send Mattie to tell Lady Margaret when my mother is ready to leave. You can leave us for now." She dismissed her with a smile and hoped she did not sound rude.

Mary only faltered for a moment but then did as she was bid. At the age of thirty-one she would have to get used to being ordered around by the new young lady. Her loyalties would always be to Lady Margaret, who gave her the position in the household after she had been widowed.

"Things are done differently here," Joan commented as she moved to stand beside her mother.

"I'd imagine so." Jeanne sounded distant, already cutting emotional ties with her daughter. She had already done this so many times in her life. First when she had left her daughters in France to marry an English nobleman, then she left her two youngest daughters to the nunnery. Now this one too was leaving her. It was the destiny of all daughters to leave for one reason or another. If Jeanne had not been careful, these constant abandonments would have broken her. Especially when she thought of the dangers she was leaving Joan to endure on her own.

Jeanne would pray her daughter would survive the trials of childbirth and that she would rise in the family's esteem.

This precious daughter would have to learn that a woman's power was given to her by a man, whoever that might be: father, husband, or even lover. While she had been given lands and inheritances, her life would be a constant battle to prove her worth. This was what she wanted to say to her daughter, what she craved for her to understand, but she would not and could not bring herself to speak. The injustice of this and her refusal to acknowledge how powerless she was herself was unfathomable.

So they spent the rest of the hour talking of Ludlow.

The pair of them sat together dining on fruit from the garden. Then Mattie appeared, saying that the carriages and the rest of the party were ready to depart.

As Mattie rushed to tell the rest of the household, Joan felt a few tears slip down her cheeks. She was furious at herself. She had not cried when she was married, and she had been so scared of that. She had not cried when her mother's mare had thrown her off her back as a child, and she had been in so much pain.

"You promised you would write to me," Jeanne reminded her daughter as they walked arm in arm to the entrance of the castle.

"I shall." Joan flicked away her tears.

"Good. Now take care and let Lady Margaret guide you. And of course, be good to that handsome husband of yours." Jeanne patted her daughter's arm. "Perhaps when you have your first child you can travel to Ludlow for your first confinement."

That seemed to brighten Joan as she thought of the future and returning to Ludlow.

Mother and daughter bid farewell on the steps of Pembridge Manor.

Roger was kind enough to take her up to the gatehouse tower to watch the party depart. He stayed with her until they disappeared into the horizon.

"They shall be safe. Father has men patrolling the forest for thieves and such." He reassured her, not quite understanding why she should be so sad.

"I know that. It simply struck me that I shall not be able to see my old home for a long time. It is odd to think that I have a new home now." She gave Roger a sad smile before she forced herself to think of other things. "Tell me of your day. How go the preparations for war?"

Roger took her hand and led her back down to the main house.

"We have begun packing to return to Wigmore. The castle is near two rivers, Teme and Lugg. There are some wonderful fishing spots and we can go rowing," Roger exclaimed, distracting his wife.

She laughed at his attempts and then realized something. "Why, the Teme flows through Ludlow! Shall we row to Ludlow, Sir Knight?"

"I had not realized." Then he stopped, and with a wave of his cap he bowed low to her. "I am at your disposal, mademoiselle. I shall row us to the end of the world if you demand it."

"Just Ludlow for now," she said, rewarding her husband with a kiss.

CHAPTER 5

1303

They had never managed to row as far as Ludlow. In those early days of marriage, the pair of them had behaved more like naughty schoolchildren. With Lord Mortimer away at war, there was no one to tell the young master no. So despite the disapproval of his mother, he carried his young bride off on adventures with his friends and her ladies.

They had races down the river, had picnics on the green, and went hunting several times.

Roger spoiled Joan mercilessly, always coming to her with a new bauble or a story. Whatever Joan commanded of her husband, a new dress or slippers, he got for her. Then at night they would take pleasure in each other's company, and Roger rarely returned to his bed until the following morning.

It was not until the winter when his father returned that they finally reined in their behavior and acted more like the adults they were supposed to be.

Margaret had disapproved, but she had lost influence over her son since she could no longer have him whipped as if he was a young boy.

JOAN

∾

Nearly two years had passed since the two were married, and the nursery had been empty for nearly a year, ever since the young Mortimer girls were sent to the nunnery.

It was then that Margaret took note of the lack of children from the seemingly happy couple. It made her begin to question Joan's fertility.

Her worries would soon be put to rest when after celebrating the New Year's feast, Joan came to her in confidence to tell her that her courses were late. The poor girl, who always acted as if she knew everything there was to know of the world, was terrified.

"Do not worry yourself," Margaret soothed her. Outside a winter storm was roaring onward. "It is bad for you and the baby."

Joan finally stopped shaking like a leaf. "Shall I tell Roger? Or is it too early?"

She knew the realities of childbirth and the fact that she might miscarry early on. She was lucky she was now seventeen and had developed fully into a woman.

"You should tell him. He should not lie with you until the babe is born. It would not be godly," Margaret warned.

Joan was about to retort, but knowing Margaret was being helpful, she nodded and promised her mother-in-law she would tell him soon. Then she remembered something.

"I wish..." For once she paused in making her demands. "To go to Ludlow for my confinement. To be with my mother. I promised her. If that would be all right?" She normally did not ask, nor did she put herself in such a vulnerable position in front of Lady Margaret.

Up until now they had been like two roosters trying to rule one roost. Both were in charge in their own way, and even though she should, Joan hardly ever gave deference to the

75

much older woman. Joan saw herself as the heir to a great fortune that had enriched this family twice over. Not only that, but she was well educated and high in her husband's favor, so she felt she deserved the title Baroness Mortimer, although she had done little to earn it. Even the servants were torn between the two ladies and their silent battles.

Now Lady Margaret had the upper hand, but she would never take advantage like that, though she wondered if Joan would do the same in her position.

"If Roger approves, I do not see why not. This is your first child, and the comfort of home will likely be a boon for you."

Joan curtsied deeply to her in thanks.

Later that day after she had calmed down, she scoured the castle until she found Roger holed up with his father discussing politics and making plans. The Scots were still posing a great threat, and there were rumors that Wales was going to rebel. If that was the case, then come spring Roger would be called to battle alongside his father.

"May I speak to you a moment?" she inquired, batting her lashes at Roger, who stood immediately and excused himself from his father's presence.

Joan pulled her husband after her down the hallway and into an alcove for more privacy.

"I have news for you."

"What is it?" Roger was impatient as always and did not appreciate her playing games.

"I am with child," she announced proudly despite her fears.

Roger's eyes bulged in surprise. In the next moment, he spun his wife around by her tiny waist before kissing her heavily.

"I guess you are pleased, non?" she inquired, laughing. The worries of childbirth were forgotten in the face of her husband's happiness.

"Yes, I am. Very much so." He looked at her suddenly as if she was very fragile and even more precious. "Do you want anything? Jewels? Dresses? Name it and I shall get it for you."

"Only to be able to go to Ludlow when it is time." She placed a hand on her belly, imagining that was where the child was growing inside of her.

Roger frowned for a moment but nodded. "If I can be spared, I shall come too. I will be there with you."

Joan laughed. "You shall be doing nothing but waiting around. I shall summon you once I go into labor. You shall be there to see the baby christened and me churched."

Roger waved her off. "It is early days to be having such arguments."

"True." She broke into another smile and could not help herself, so she kissed his cheek. "Now go back to your father before he thinks you have abandoned him again."

Roger rolled his eyes but did as he was bid.

He still had a childish disposition to avoid responsibilities whenever he could. As the spoiled heir, his parents hardly ever corrected him. They trusted he would learn with time.

∼

Winter deepened, but the happiness around Wigmore Castle was undisturbed. Joan was progressing well with her pregnancy. The morning sickness had lasted a mere month, and under the tender care of her husband she flourished.

Once the weather seemed to steady and the sun illuminated the snow-covered landscape, Joan finally sent a messenger to her mother telling her the news and asking if she might come in the summer for her confinement. There was a lot to do, it seemed, to welcome a baby. Midwives and tapestries, relics and holy girdles had to be arranged. It was all too strange for her.

So instead she spent much of her time in her solar with her own ladies, holding court as they made clothes for the arriving baby, sewed shirts for her husband and father-in-law, and talked of gossip that came from the king's court.

"They say his son Edward is a handsome man," the daughter of a squire commented wistfully, dreaming of a prince to marry her. As if such a thing were possible.

As one of the ladies of the house, Joan should have corrected her and taught her ladies more decorum, but she herself was young and foolishly in love. She loved to think of love matches and found scandalous affairs entertaining.

"If only you had a bigger dowry to tempt him," she teased her lady-in-waiting.

"Oh, I think she has a big enough endowment to catch his eye." Another lady made a bawdy joke referring to the previous lady's chest, which strained against her dress though she had a slender waist.

Joan scolded her for such jokes. There was a line that even she would not cross. She did not want it going around that she talked like a barmaid and had crude manners.

"Let's leave poor Felicia alone," she suggested before turning the topic. "Has there been any news from Scotland or France?"

"Not that I have heard of, milady." Felicia looked away, disappointed she did not have an answer.

One of the young ladies whose mother was serving at the king's court had more to tell. "I heard King Edward is mounting his final invasion of Scotland. That brute Bruce will be captured and soundly defeated no doubt, with France once more on our side."

Joan bit her lip. While it was good news that victory and an end to the war were finally on the horizon, she knew that this news meant that Roger would be riding out. All of autumn he had ridden in a mock joust with his friends, practicing his cavalry charge and his skills with the sword. She had watched with pride but also felt that this was no game. She could not smile as he and Simon dueled. Every time Roger lost, every time he was nicked with a sword, all she could imagine was that in war there would be no stopping. There would be no friendly face helping him get up after he had fallen into the dirt.

She prayed with a certain hopelessness she had never felt before. Perhaps it was her condition that made her feel so scared. She dearly wished she could ride out with him and protect him from any folly. Joan knew with his foolish pride he would put himself in great danger to prove to the world he was a brave, strong man.

"Pray to God the fighting ends and that the king is victorious."

"Amen," the room replied, and they turned to happier topics.

As spring approached, there was news from London. Baron Mortimer was to attend parliament and help muster the troops in the Welsh Marshes. Additionally, Roger would go with him and he would help his father lead the battalion.

After dinner that night, when the sun had set, Lord Mortimer approached Joan. "You shall have to write to your mother to begin mustering troops for our campaign and to send supplies. Ludlow and its lands are yours now, and we need more men."

"Are we in great danger?" Joan inquired. From gossip she had heard it seemed as if the Scots were entirely beaten back and that victory was assured.

Edmund Mortimer smiled at her innocence, but these were serious matters. "There is trouble in Wales, and the Scots are always popping up like weeds. We need to be prepared, but there is no reason for you to fear. You shall remain here with my lady wife and shall be safe behind the walls of Wigmore."

Joan nodded and tried to play the part of the placated young woman. But she knew, for Master Banner had taught her that battles were never assured, there was no safety in war and no matter how hard you planned, something as simple as the sun shining in your eyes might tip the scales against you. The king must be worried indeed if he was mustering from all over the country. It would be worse still if Wales rebelled now with his attention on Scotland.

From whispers she overheard, she knew that the king had fallen out of favor with his subjects, from his heavy taxation to increasing brutality against all who opposed him. Joan knew better than to repeat such gossip or make her own opinions known, but in her heart she frowned at what the king was doing.

To the outward world, she was a mute obedient wife with no opinions of her own.

But that did not mean she would not listen, that she would remain ignorant. She would find ways to protect her husband in her own little ways. Master Banner had taught her that knowledge was power. If she could gather knowledge about her opponent, then she would know how to defeat him or how to keep his friendship and gain his trust.

They were valuable lessons that she was learning, and she quickly learned that by flattering her father-in-law and entertaining him with songs and dances he came to admire her as a sweet girl who he could trust with his thoughts, which was how she gained much of her information.

To her husband, she challenged him. Raced horses with him, helped him with his accounts, and was there to placate him with kisses and tender embraces. He saw a worthy partner

JOAN

in her and enjoyed that, unlike his mother, she seemed strong and ambitious.

She could be one of the boys but much more precious than any of them, for she was carrying his child now.

Joan's relationship with Lady Margaret had become friendlier ever since she announced her pregnancy. She would pad off to her rooms and sit with her, discussing her symptoms and asking her advice.

The lady seemed to enjoy the company and being given the respect she was due. She had all but retired from her duties, seeing as Joan was capable. It was as if after her daughters and other children had left she no longer had a purpose. Her husband seemed to be constantly at war, and they had fallen out of touch with each other. Of course, he paid her every respect, but they were hardly ever alone together as man and wife.

As the snows thawed, Joan's letters to her mother were being exchanged with more frequency. Lists of provisions, numbers of yeomen, and the small army that was mustered was accounted for in all the letters as well as the cost of everything. The treasury of England was depleted, but parliament had promised Lord Mortimer that they would be compensated once Scotland was taken.

Her belly was growing large and Joan hoped it was a boy. In a few months, she would make the journey to Ludlow as she was promised, provided that the roads were safe.

Then one night in early May a rider in the night wearing the livery of King Edward himself came riding up to the gates of Wigmore Castle. "An urgent message!" he cried, waking the household servants.

The steward immediately pounced on the letter and seeing the seal, woke his master, who was slumbering.

Lord Mortimer, who was in his fifties, grumbled at being

awoken so. Stiffly, he hurried down the stairs to greet the messenger.

As she was instructed to do, Joan's maid Abigale came to tell her the news despite the late hour.

Joan was quick on her feet. Roger was not with her this night, and she was grateful he was not here to see her gracelessly plodding around the room getting dressed. She covered her dark hair in a simple net and coif. She wrapped a thick fur around her and with Abigale at her side went to the great hall to hear the news.

Lord Mortimer was assuring the messenger that the king's demands would be met and sent him on his way with a purse heavy with coin. They would defend the north, though they were ill-prepared at the moment. They had not thought a war would come so quickly.

Seeing his daughter-in-law peering at him, he plopped himself into a nearby chair as exhaustion hit him. "Wales has risen up."

That was all Joan needed to know. They were now at war.

"I shall write to my mother's steward immediately. They shall be here within the week. Shall I send for some mulled wine for you, my lord?" She was ever attentive and quick to help.

"Thank you, and send me my steward. We shall have to pack." Then coyly he added, "And see if you can wake that husband of yours. It's time for him to show his worth. He should be here, not his pregnant wife."

She smiled kindly at him before running to do as she was bid.

Joan sent Abigale to find the steward and to tell Master Banner to come to her husband's rooms.

"Darling?" Roger muttered groggily when she shook him awake.

"There was news. We are to go to war. You must rise and

get ready to help your father." At her words, he jumped out of bed, suddenly alert.

He ran about the room trying to get dressed and calling out things he needed to bring with him.

Joan watched him with amusement until he stilled and came to her with an embarrassed grin.

"My mind is running amok. I shall send my groomsmen to fetch my armor and have the servants ready my things. I should talk to Father." He kissed her nose. "Will you be all right? You are not frightened, are you?"

Joan shook her head. All winter she had thought of little else. Everyone seemed assured of their victory and she had prayed many days on her knees for God to watch over her family. "I am quite resolved to have you back by my side in August and for you to hold our little boy." She placed his hand over her belly and he felt the babe kick.

"My brave little wife." He placed a kiss on her lips and with that ran out of the room.

Joan did not return to bed just yet, although she was tired and her condition was wearing her down. She had to make sure everything was just right. Walking to the opposite end of the castle, she went to her mother-in-law's room. Her servants had awoken her and she had gone to chapel to pray.

She knelt beside Lady Margaret and placed a hand on her shoulder. "We shall be victorious," she swore, though in truth she was no wise woman who foresaw the future.

"Praise be to God," the tired woman replied.

"Do you require anything?"

She shook her head. No.

Joan then returned to her own rooms. Master Banner and his assistant were there. They had heard the news that had spread throughout the castle like wildfire.

"I have already written out the letters, my lady. All they need is your signature."

Joan thanked him. Skimming the letters, she signed with a quick flourish. "Make sure they are sent immediately."

He handed them to his assistant, who ran off.

"You have grown in the time I've known you."

Joan bowed her head in thanks at the compliment, and he disappeared from her rooms, knowing he had much work to do. She had given him the position as her personal steward, and while as of yet he did not have much responsibility other than overseeing her other servants and ensuring the lands awarded to her by her grandfather were being maintained, he was still constantly busy. She also relied on him as a valued adviser, and she did not wish to lose him just yet. Besides, she envisioned that at some point he would tutor her own children.

The next day Joan had to stand tall as she bid Lord Mortimer and her husband farewell. They had a guard of twenty men and they would ride around their lands mustering troops and arming men. Already wagons of supplies were being arranged and would be sent after them.

"Send word to me." Joan took Roger's hands in hers. "And take care of yourself."

He smiled at her as if she was a child who knew nothing. "Do not fret, my love." Out of his pocket, he pulled out a brooch. It was a prancing lion embossed in gold, holding in its great paws a large sapphire encircled by diamonds. Blue for the Mortimer crest. "Be brave like an English lioness." He was going to give her this once the child was born but felt that now was as good a time as any.

Joan smiled in thanks at the keepsake and gave him a kiss. He knelt before his mother for her blessing and then was off, jumping on his horse and riding through the gatehouse with his father, leading their men away.

"God, keep them safe," Lady Margaret said in a voice so faint Joan barely heard her.

"Amen. Come, let us go inside." Joan led her by the hand.

Over the next few weeks, there was little for them to do but pray and go about their business as usual. There was little news from the north.

They had engaged the Welsh, joined by other noblemen and their armies, while the king with his royal army had entered Scotland. It seemed wherever you turned there was fighting and war. The villagers and peasants were ill at ease. They harbored countless terrors from more taxes to failing crops, to armies that would pillage and raid what little they had left. Even this far south they feared that the Scots might rally and bring their horrors upon them.

Joan had to straighten her back and as petitioners appeared at the castle doors for news or asking for sanctuary, she had to keep a cool head and ensure she did not get swallowed up by what she knew as hollow worries.

Lady Margaret had taken to her bed with a fever. Joan would have cursed her had she not been sending instructions in a constant stream to all the servants of the castle. They were to send the necessary provisions while trying to store anything they could in case there was a siege. For all of Joan's knowledge, she had never lived through warfare and never had the running of a whole castle to manage.

Together the two women managed to weather the storm. When June arrived, there were increasing amounts of good news, from the Welsh being pushed back to victories in Scotland. Finally, Margaret felt it was safe to send Joan to Ludlow.

A litter was prepared for her and a guard was arranged to see her along her journey safely.

"Stop only at the abbeys or ask for room at castles. Inns won't be safe if there is an attack," Margaret warned her just in case.

Joan, who was now heavy with child and increasingly in a

bad mood, nodded quickly. She wanted to leave now and so would not argue with the matriarch.

"Godspeed." Margaret kissed both her cheeks, and a servant boy helped Joan step into the litter.

∼

The journey, which had taken her a mere three days to make as a young girl three years previously, now took nearly a week.

When Joan spotted the familiar row of thatched roofs and the imposing red stone walls of Ludlow, she gave a cry of joy.

Many of the villagers turned out when they heard her arrival and came out to greet the small party, curious to see their mistress who had finally come home again.

Joan waved to all the friendly faces, who shouted blessings upon her as was customary.

Her mother was waiting to greet her as they finally stopped in the courtyard. Both women bowed to each other and held their arms together in greeting before Jeanne announced that they would go inside and eat.

Joan stared at her mother as she commanded the servants to prepare the confinement chamber to her specifications. She had barely changed, but there were new lines crossing her face that had not been there before and gray hairs peeking out of her hood, but she remained the same strong woman Joan knew.

"You shall have the very best of care," Jeanne reassured her daughter, who she was surprised to see was still small and petite, only changed by the round belly and new plumpness around her face. "I thought you would grow a bit taller," she mentioned as she led her daughter to sit by the fire.

"Alas, it was not to be." Joan knew she would never be one of those tall majestic ladies from stories, but she did not mind, for when Roger looked at her she knew she was loved. "My husband is now almost two heads taller than me. I look like a dwarf beside him." She laughed.

"I doubt it." Jeanne shook her head, disbelieving. "Your presence alone would make up the difference. You will find Ludlow unchanged. If you are feeling up for it, I can show you the new garden I had planted the year you left us. Your grandparents are well and surprisingly spry." Jeanne caught up Joan on the family news.

"And what of my sisters?"

Jeanne scrunched up her nose. "They are well enough. Maud still writes to me weekly complaining of this and that. Beatrice is quite an obedient novice and I am told she will soon take her vows."

"That is wonderful. She seemed happy there. Half of Wigmore was sent to the church. Their mother has a way of instilling the desire to serve God in them. Perhaps Maud would benefit." Joan choked back a laugh, for she did not wish to make fun of her mother-in-law.

At the end of the week, after Joan had been spoiled rotten to the point where all she wanted to do was lie in bed all day, she finally entered her confinement. The dark room quickly soured her mood, and she wished she would not have to endure this for long.

As she waited, Jeanne received troubling news from Wigmore Castle. Lord Edmund Mortimer was dead. Injured on the battlefield, he made it home before passing away. Roger, still considered in minority, was given in guardianship to Gaveston, the Prince of Wales's favorite. What this meant Jeanne could only guess, but she would keep it from Joan, who was already in a foul temper. She thanked God Joan's husband had been spared and that now her daughter was a baroness.

A rising star in the world.

A week before the end of July and attended by midwives and her mother, Joan went into labor. The pains came hard and fast, but within four hours she was delivered of a healthy baby girl with dark hair and green eyes like her mother.

Joan, who was weeping as she held her baby both from exhaustion and happiness, was told that she was lucky that her childbirth went so easily.

"Truly, Mother?" Joan asked as her mother wiped the sweat from her brow.

"Oh yes. I labored with you for three days. You were a stubborn baby. Perhaps you have been blessed to have an easy time. Next you shall have a son," Jeanne predicted.

Joan nodded, for she had felt the pang of disappointment when the midwife had announced it was a girl. She felt sorry for her immediately and hoped the babe knew she was loved regardless. It was just that she had imagined she was carrying a boy...perhaps she would only have girls like her mother. The image of the perfect family seemed lost to her for now.

"What shall you call this little one?" Jeanne asked. She cooed to the little baby, who had finished suckling.

"Margaret, after Roger's mother." Joan thought for a moment. "Then we shall have another babe named after you too, Mother. I promise."

Jeanne laughed. "Don't worry, I am not insulted, but I am sure your mother-in-law will be pleased. Now, ma chérie, before I go to write a letter to your husband I must tell you some grave news."

Joan immediately jumped to attention, weariness disappearing from her face as she concentrated. "What is it?"

"Unfortunately, Lord Mortimer has died from injuries in battle. Your husband is safe and sound and you are now a baroness."

Joan crossed herself at the news. "May he rest in peace."

"Yes. That is also why your husband is not yet by your

side. There was much to do, as I can imagine. Once the baby has been christened and you have been churched, I am sure he will come to fetch you himself. There are some legal matters involving guardianship over Roger and you," Jeanne continued.

"What do you mean? Roger is old enough now at seventeen. He is green but old enough." Joan frowned. "Who?"

"Gaveston, the king's favorite. We must bow our heads and accept this. Besides, it won't be for long. I predict it shall only last for three years at most."

After a few days, when Joan felt she had fully recovered, she wrote a long letter to her husband, asking him for news of Wigmore and to send condolences to his mother on her behalf. She asked him what this all meant with his inheritance and what he would do in the meantime.

She received a reply that he was to go to court and appear before parliament to see if they would relent and give him his letters patent and be sworn to the king. He would send her a present, he promised.

Joan sighed. Did he think all she wanted was presents? But that was how Roger showed his affection and how he liked to remind her she was in his thoughts. Joan sometimes wondered if he was the more romantic of the two of them.

∼

Within the month, Joan had been churched with Lady Margaret and her mother at her side, for she had come to witness the christening of Roger's first child.

Together they traveled back to Wigmore Castle in an even more extravagant litter piled high with furs and cushions.

"My son spoils you." Lady Margaret sniffed, but she did not seem to mind the added comfort on the journey.

Finally, after a few more days, Joan and Roger were reunited.

Joan leaped into his arms, forgetting all decorum, and presented his daughter to him.

"She is ours?" he asked, beaming at the little creature.

Joan nodded. "All ours."

"I am so glad to have you home. It has been quite lonely without you, Baroness." He added her title for a flourish and was pleased to see her flush with excitement at her rise in station.

The pair entered the castle hand in hand, their daughter carried in by the nursemaid behind them.

A family made whole again.

CHAPTER 6

1306

Her mother's predictions were accurate. It took three years for her and Roger to shake off Gaveston and his guardianship. He had walked away with over two thousand marks as fees for one thing or another. He made excuses such as the fact that he had not given permission for Roger to marry Joan, although they had been married for three years already and had a baby in the cradle and another on the way.

Joan urged Roger to petition the king, but of course he sided with his son's favorite.

Lady Margaret, who was playing with her namesake, swinging her back and forth, said that they should be glad they were not fined for complaining and now they were free and all of Roger's lands were restored to him.

Joan knew they should be grateful, but she could not help the treasonous thoughts that the king was unjustly claiming money that was not his. Like a grubby moneylender, he impoverished his subjects to fill his treasury so he could reward his favorites.

Joan swore she would not go to court, although as Roger told her frequently, that was how you rose up in the world.

It was after the May Day celebrations, where Joan had been crowned the May Queen as Roger placed a crown of flowers on her head, when a messenger arrived.

Roger came bounding into her rooms unannounced and uncharacteristically cheerful. "We shall go to London. I shall be knighted alongside the Prince of Wales for my service in Wales and Scotland."

Joan clapped her hands together in surprise. "That is wonderful news."

"Will you come with me?" he asked, knowing of the promise she had sworn.

With a shy grin, she replied, "I suppose I could make an exception."

Roger paused in his joy for a moment. "Do you think it will be safe with the baby?"

"I believe so. There are still three months to go, and I shall be back here for my confinement." As if hearing they were talking of it, the baby kicked in the womb and Joan placed a hand over her belly.

"Roger, I would wish to call the baby Matilda if it is a girl after my grandmother, God rest her soul, if you would not object." Her grandmother had passed away two years ago and she was still saddened by the loss.

"Of course." Roger nodded. "And if it's a boy?"

"Edmund, after your father."

Roger liked the sound of that and came and knelt by her side. "That would be a great honor. I am sure my mother will be pleased and spoil him silly." He stood once more. "You shall order a few more dresses and you will see to it that plans are made for our departure, won't you?"

"Yes, I shall. Now off with you. I am sure there will be a tournament and you will want to practice your jousting, Baron Mortimer."

"Baroness." He tipped his cap to her and with a wink left her rooms.

The ladies-in-waiting around her immediately began chattering about the news. They looked hopefully at Joan to declare they would be coming as well. At court, they might catch the eye of a great lord, and the famous feasts and dances made them quiver with anticipation.

Joan, who was now in her twenties and married for five years, had still not lost her childish exuberance for such things either.

"What say you, ladies? Shall you attend to me in London?"

"Oh yes!" came the chorus almost immediately.

The ladies laughed as they put aside their sewing and talked of the dresses they would wear and the men they would meet. They would even be able to catch a glimpse of the king!

Joan arranged their departure with Lady Margaret at her side. She would stay back and safeguard their lands, make sure the farmers planted a healthy crop and that the servants did not slack off in their work. She would also look after the three-year-old Margaret, who everyone called Maggie.

Maggie was the one thing Joan was loath to leave behind. She was a sweet little girl, with bright shining eyes, and clever.

Already she was talking French, and Joan would soon find a tutor to teach her English and Latin.

∽

With the litters prepared, horses saddled, and wagons carrying their chests of clothes and supplies loaded up, the large party of ten men, five ladies-in-waiting, and other servants, as well as guards, set out for London.

Roger, still the loving husband, rode beside Joan's litter to converse with her from time to time.

She wished for the freedom to ride alongside him, but, of

course, her condition prevented it. Dressed in finery, she regarded his friends with jealousy as they captured his attention with bawdy jokes and fantastical tales.

As they neared London, he was no longer by her side but at the head of the party.

Joan was curious how everyone was to be housed and where their horses and things would go, but the king's chamberlain, who greeted them at the Palace of Westminster, merely bowed to them and snapped his fingers. Like clockwork, servants appeared to help unload the wagons, the groomsmen led the horses to the stables, and they were shown to their rooms.

They were to be honored guests, and while they were not given rooms close to the king's, they received lordly accommodations.

Soon after her arrival, her loyal maidservant Abigale knocked at her private chamber. "There is a messenger from the queen."

Joan stood up as quickly as her condition allowed. "Show him in."

The liveried servant strode in, bowing, and gave her the message that she was invited to wait upon the young queen and keep her company.

"I would be honored and shall come as soon as I am changed," Joan promised.

The servant bowed and retreated just as quickly as he had arrived.

"Send for Lady Felicia to help me with my headdress and pull out the azure silk gown. I shall not go before the queen looking like a pauper," Joan ordered Abigale as she began untying her traveling cloak from her shoulders. "And see if you can send word to Roger as to where I have gone, if he remembers that he has a wife." She joked, for he had run off to greet

JOAN

the other young men who were to be knighted alongside him and she was quite forgotten.

An hour later—finally dressed with her hair tucked into neat braids under a gold caul, a sheer veil pinned over the top, and her strings of pearls hanging from her neck—she finally left her rooms and headed to the queen's quarters, led by a servant sent for the task.

The queen's rooms were lavishly decorated with brilliant tapestries. On the wall, numerous amounts of candles were lit, adding a brilliant light. On an equally magnificent chair sat the queen, surrounded by her ladies. Other servants stood around the room, ready to be of service the minute they were called.

Her eyes watched as Joan entered, sliding to her protruding belly.

Joan dipped into a deep curtsy in the presence of her majesty, surprising herself that she was able to keep from wobbling.

"Rise, Lady Joan," the queen greeted her. Her accent was still heavily French. "You are welcome to court. I am glad to make your acquaintance."

Joan bobbed another curtsy and thanked her profusely.

Queen Margaret motioned for one of her ladies to move aside so that Joan might take a seat beside her. "Sit with me."

They spent much time talking together of pleasantries. Queen Margaret herself was pregnant with her third child, but she was only four months along.

"There will be a grand feast and celebrations for days afterward. The king has finally decided to knight his son and picked out several other young men too. I do hope you shall attend me, and we shall become great friends."

Joan could only nod. This woman was so much greater than herself. She marveled at her splendor and easy grace.

This was a true queen.

Only six years older than herself, Queen Margaret was

never crowned officially. She was the second wife, and while she had finally come into her husband's favor, King Edward was not disposed to honor her in this way. Still, Margaret commanded every respect and was still called queen. In her short years of marriage, she had given the king two more boy heirs, who she doted on. However, instead of favoring them and trying to push them forward, she instead worked to solidify the relationship between her husband and her stepson. Both men tended to be at each other's throat, and the whole court was grateful for her calming influence.

Eventually, the small court around the queen arose, sensing it was time for dinner.

Following behind some of the more important ladies of the court, Joan took her place in the procession line to dinner.

As they walked into the grand dining hall, she kept an eye out for Roger. She saw him, Simon at his side and Hugh, the Earl of Herford, at his other. She gave him a small wave from across the room and he returned it with a smile.

Musicians played as the food was brought out on plates of polished silver. The king and queen sitting on the dais with the royal children, who were old enough to eat with the court, were presented with very fine dishes. After tasting them, they passed them along to their favorites.

Queen Margaret, who did not forget Lady Joan was new to court, favored her by sending her a dish of duck stewed with plums and sweet dates.

The food seemed unending, and the conversation around her was streaming so fast it was impossible for Joan to keep track of it. The ladies on either side of her did not pay much attention to her, and Joan felt out of her element and dazzled by the whole affair.

She had always considered Ludlow the finest of places, but it seemed like a backcountry manor house now.

After the feasting, acrobats streamed in, the court fool

made jokes that sent everyone laughing, and then of course there was dancing.

It was nearing midnight and the court was still awake. The old king was clearly drowsy in his seat but refused to admit he was tired. Queen Margaret was at his side, whispering to her husband to keep him entertained.

Joan was finally feeling her energy draining from her and she wished to retire.

Slowly, she made her way to Roger, who was standing around with his friends watching ladies dancing about.

"Lord husband," she began with a tired smile to him. "I wish to retire. Shall you see me to our rooms?"

Roger looked a bit disappointed, but he would not abandon her. "Of course."

He bid farewell to the other young men and walked out of the hall with her.

"Is the baby well?" he asked, returning to being the doting husband that he was.

"Oh yes, but the journey and the court have sapped all the energy out of me. I do not know if I should ever get used to the opulence."

"You will." He grinned. "Perhaps if you befriend the queen, she will ask you to be one of her ladies."

"Perhaps," Joan replied, though she had no intention of doing so just yet. She liked being mistress of her own domain in her own home. She realized she was not ready nor was she ambitious enough to live at court.

Roger joined her in bed, climbing in under the covers and sighing as his weary bones finally rested.

"Are you an old man now?" Joan jested beside him.

"Only very tired." He leaned over and gave her a tender kiss. "You were right to pull me away this night. Tomorrow will be a long day; the Prince of Wales wishes to go hunting."

Joan nodded, knowing that this meant she would be alone

once more tomorrow. She had not realized how lucky she had been that they had so much time together at Wigmore Castle. How greedily she would seek to keep him by her side.

"Ma chérie, I know you are nervous at court. Where is the brave young lady I married? The lady who has the command of the whole of Herefordshire should not balk at this new challenge." He scolded her, though his tone was more encouraging and loving than his words.

"You are right. I shall try harder." Joan gave a big yawn and lay back against her pillow. "Good night."

It was funny how quickly things could change in a few days.

Joan took her husband's encouragement to heart and walked head held high into the queen's chambers. She did not act as if she was superior to the ladies there, but nor did she act as though she was unworthy to be here at court. She was a baroness by marriage and a great heiress by birth, descended from the great houses of de Geneville and Lusignan, a royal French family. She was not some upstart unsure of her position in life.

While Joan befriended the other ladies and conversed with the queen, Roger was now the one having difficulties.

He complained often to her at night, whispering that the Prince of Wales favored one man above all others.

"I won the horse race yesterday and was supposed to win the purse, but the prince declared that I had cheated somehow and that Gaveston was the winner of the day." He huffed, pacing their rooms. Joan looked to their groomsmen and maidservants standing around the room, awaiting instruction.

She was wary of what they might report should someone ask. They were under their employment, but that did not mean they would not gossip that Baron Mortimer was no friend of the Prince of Wales.

Placing a steadying hand on her husband, she urged him

not to take this to heart. "Your pride is injured. Perhaps you did get a head start in the race and did not realize it. I know how excited you can get." He was about to argue, but then he saw her pointed stare and caught on.

He gave a laugh.

"My God, you are right. I am always impulsive and hotheaded. I shall confess my sinfulness tomorrow after mass." Then he turned to the servants and dismissed them for the night. "It is time we go to bed," he announced.

After they had finally been left alone, tucked into their warm bed. Roger placed his head to hers.

"Ma chérie, you are thinking like a courtier. What would I do without you?"

They spoke in hushed tones.

"I look out for our family, nothing more. But I am glad you are happy with me."

He gave a little sigh. "I am still angry about today. There seems to be no room for me at court. All favors go to Gaveston. The king is too old and weary now to take much heart to this. Though Hugh told me that just last year he had fought viciously with his son over his favoritism. He said it was an ungodly love."

"What?" Joan hissed, horrified to hear such a thing.

"Only the good queen's intervention helped them reconcile. I hate to think what will happen when Prince Edward takes the throne. They say he would give all of England to Gaveston." Roger spoke this last part even softer, lest they were somehow overheard.

Joan crossed herself. Would England fall into another civil war? The people were already so unhappy. All she prayed for was peace. "Let us talk no more of this. Soon we shall be away from this place and the politics."

Roger nodded and lay down, taking his wife's hand in his, and fell asleep.

In the days leading up to the great ceremony, more and more people were streaming into court. There was hardly an empty room at Westminster Palace.

It was estimated over two hundred men were to be knighted and given rewards. Every day there were new entertainments, from a bear baiting to a tourney to a hunt in which the old king himself rode a great stallion.

Joan thought of how ancient King Edward looked, but still he had his wits about him and could handle his horse with great skill. She thought of her grandfather, who was still ruling at Trim Castle and who was six years older than him and still going strong. Other men had crumpled with age, but these two seemed as if they would go on forever.

"Will you sit with me and tell me of the Welsh Marches?" Queen Margaret asked her one day as the ladies of the court sat outside under a willow tree, waiting for the men to return from their latest hunting expedition.

With the queen pregnant, she would not ride out on such strenuous rides, though it was rumored she had been out hunting when she went into labor with her first child.

Joan stood and sat down beside her a respectable distance away. "It is a very beautiful country. We are not so far north that the weather is gloomy. The land is lush and we have many orchards and farmland. My own mother planted a rose garden that flourishes beautifully at Ludlow."

"Sounds like a wonderful place."

Joan nodded but then like a courtier added, "Of course, it does not even compare to the beauty of London and the Thames River.

"We shall have to get the men to take us rowing tomorrow."

JOAN

"That would be exciting," Lady Alice jumped in. "We should make them race with the barges."

Queen Margaret chuckled. "It has become such an energetic court. I shall tell the chamberlain to arrange it."

The trumpets sounding off in the distance announced the return of the hunting party.

The ladies twittered in anticipation and set about arranging their skirts, tucking pieces of loose hair back into their caps, or sitting up straight. They hoped to catch the attention of the unmarried Prince of Wales or any of the other eligible bachelors.

As the party approached, Joan noticed for the first time how some of the ladies giggled at the handsome sight of her husband astride his horse. Their eyes watched as he dismounted, and he in turn played the courteous courtier, giving innocent smiles to each of them.

Then as the king dismounted, the ladies stood curtsying low with their heads bent to the ground. After the familiar etiquette was conducted, the king took his queen's hand and led her to the grand table that had been set up to feed the party.

Cooks had been cooking over open fires, roasting freshly caught rabbits and birds for their meal.

Joan walked up to her husband, a hand on her protruding belly as she stood proudly beside him. Then, as he led her to her seat at the table, she made sure that all could see she was staking her claim to him.

For his part, Roger seemed quite innocent in the attention he was getting. He only seemed to have eyes for his wife. After all, he had more pressing matters to think of than catching the attention of a beauty. He wished to find some way to gain favor at court, and he was sure that would not happen through the skirts of a lady.

The next day, as the queen had promised, there was a day

of rowing. The ladies were floating slowly down the river in comfortable barges while the men raced in competition with each other. Minstrels played at the edge of the river, which alternated with the sounds of drumming coming from the rowers.

Joan and Roger retired laughing and in good spirits that night.

"I could get used to this," Joan whispered to him as they lay down beside each other.

"It's not all fun and games," Roger warned. But for all of his protests he too was thriving in the festivities and exuberance of court.

"Are you nervous for tomorrow?"

Roger would be knighted at Westminster Abbey tomorrow while Joan watched from the sidelines, silently cheering him on. His groomsmen had already prepared his pure-white robes, gold lace stripes covering the tunic. All the men had been commanded to dress accordingly. This would be the Feast of the Swans. Roger had told her that they would be swearing fealty to two white swans, the king and the prince.

Joan, to match her husband, had ordered a gown of yellow silk to be made. Her husband's blue crest was embroidered into the bottom of her gown and down the length of her magnificent sleeves. It was quite an expense, but Roger had not even batted an eye at the price when he had seen her in it.

"You shall outshine everyone at court." He had complimented her.

In the gown, she looked the very picture of fertility and beauty. The perfect wife.

The ceremony was just as grand as any of the other festivities. White roses hung from the rafters of the abbey and lute players played a soft melody.

The king looked grand as he stood at the center of the church in front of the giant gold cross.

JOAN

One by one the men were called before him. They took a knee in front of their monarch and swore their fealty as they were touched by the sword and given their letters patent by a servant standing nearby.

Joan beamed as Roger stood before the king. They would finally be coming into their own.

After the feasting and dancing were concluded, the pair sat on their beds, reading over all the lands that were now theirs.

"These are all mine," Roger declared. Joan did not even bother to correct him.

"So many manor houses and castles." She choked after seeing them all listed before her. Pembridge, Flint, Ludlow, Wigmore Castle, and many more.

"Yes, we shall have many towns and places to look after. Perhaps we can even get a house in London. I am sure we can afford it." He had plans of staying at court or visiting often.

While Joan did miss the countryside and her familiar home, she could not complain about this. She too was addicted to life at court. There was never a dull moment.

By the end of the week, though, they had to pack up and return home. There were no more excuses that could be made.

Joan took her leave of the queen and wished her good health and luck in the remainder of her pregnancy.

"I hope we shall be seeing more of each other," Queen Margaret graciously complimented her.

"If my lord husband should allow."

～

As they rode back to Wigmore Castle, Joan wished to hear all the gossip from her ladies. Had any men caught their attention? Was there any scandal to be heard that she had not caught a whiff of?

It was then she heard that the king was in talks with France to arrange the marriage of his son. All the ladies were understandably disappointed.

Lady Margaret Mortimer was waiting for them at the gates of Wigmore as the party rode up in good spirits.

At first Joan was fearful that she had bad news for them, but her sour expression quickly melted away to a smile at the sight of her son.

"You grow more like your father every day." She greeted him, then kissed Joan on both cheeks. "How well you both look."

She paused a moment, taking them in.

"Come, Maggie is waiting for you patiently in the hall, and I have a dinner prepared for you."

Joan watched as her little daughter, who had just learned to walk a mere year ago, dipped into an awkward curtsy to greet her father and mother.

She laughed and clapped her hands in happiness at the sight. Roger, who doffed his cap to her, quickly picked her up and spun her around.

Maggie screamed in glee. This was her favorite game to play with her father.

With his daughter still in his arms, Roger brought her to Joan. "What a pretty little lady we have here. She shall turn quite a few heads."

"This ugly thing," Joan teased, caressing her daughter's soft hair.

"I'm not ugly." Maggie pouted. She looked like she was ready to throw a tantrum already.

Joan frowned. It would not do to raise a daughter full of temper and disobedience. "I think you are ready to be sent to your rooms for the night. Be a good girl and say your prayers."

Maggie's nurse stepped forward and took the child from her father's arms.

"You should not be too harsh with her." Roger was ever the indulgent father.

"She knows I love her, but I will not tolerate bad behavior either. Besides, one of us needs to be the disciplinarian, and I don't believe you have the heart for it."

"You unman me, madam!" He placed a hand over his heart as if she had struck him a blow.

Joan rolled her eyes at his antics. "Come. Let us join your mother and eat. I grow tired and this babe is fussing." The child in her belly was kicking anxiously. "I shall bet you a crown he comes early."

Her words proved to be an accurate prediction, for she had barely begun her confinement when her waters broke. She feared the babe would be sickly being born so early, but while a bit small, she had given birth to a healthy baby boy, who they called Edmund.

Roger finally had an heir. The family was ecstatic.

The christening pulled in relatives from all over the country. Joan's own mother made the trip, and her grandfather sent her father's christening gown for the new heir.

Throughout this, little Maggie was quite put out. She was no longer the only child. Now she had a little brother who everyone seemed to dote on more than they ever paid attention to her. Secretly she prayed at night that there would be no more children to have to share her parents with.

Unfortunately, God had not been listening.

CHAPTER 7

1308

The bells were pealing once more throughout the countryside. This time in celebration.

King Edward I had died on the seventh of July, 1307.

Now, in the heart of winter, King Edward II was married to Princess Isabella of France.

The country was reborn, and in the New Year there was much to celebrate.

Pacing her chamber as her labor pangs abated, Joan's thoughts were not of her own condition but of Roger, who had been invited to the wedding celebrations.

Just last summer both she and Roger had traveled to London to witness the coronation of King Edward II. Putting aside their mourning for the deceased king, they had feasted and celebrated with the young monarch. He was tall, handsome, and athletic. The very image of a gracious king.

Joan had been reunited with the dowager Queen Margaret while she was there.

She had given birth to a daughter shortly before her husband's death. For her whole marriage, she had served him well and with a loving heart, but she had always played second fiddle to a beloved deceased wife.

"How the wheel turns, Lady Mortimer." The dark blue gown she wore made her look sickly. Joan realized then that Margaret truly loved King Edward, though he had been much older than herself and had never had her anointed. How strange love was.

"What will you do now?" she had asked.

"I shall stay as long as my stepson needs me. I assume he shall be married soon. Then I can retire to Marlborough Castle."

Joan looked around to the other ladies, who were equally aghast. It was she who finally spoke up, trying to put it tactfully.

"You are still young, Your Grace." She choked.

"Ah, there was one man for me and now he is gone. None other shall take his place."

Joan bowed under her gaze.

The conversation was stilted after that. The ladies continued with their sewing for the coronation and tried to be merry, though they were all turned upside down by the death of the king. Their positions at court could no longer be assured, and soon there would be a new queen with new demands and preferences.

Thinking back to her time in London got Joan through the bleak dreary days in confinement.

She had never been at such a glamorous event before. It overshadowed the Feast of the Swans tenfold and had much more importance.

The midwives were bringing in linen and trying to get a bigger fire going in the room.

Even though she was only twenty-three, Joan already felt like a seasoned veteran of childbirth. She had a feeling that this baby would be in no rush to come out in this blasted cold weather.

There had been an unending stream of storms ever since Roger left. She wished he could be with her now to tell her of the queen's coronation and wedding. It was rumored that she was quite beautiful and quick-witted. If it was true, then the royal couple would make a beautiful pair, and she prayed their union would be a happy one.

Roger spoke daily of the outrage of the favoritism shown to Gaveston, but Joan would tease him that he also favored Maggie above everyone else. She was his darling little girl, even though she was no heir.

"It's not the same." He seemed exasperated with her but then apologized right away for his tone. "I..."

"You are ambitious and wish to have some favor bestowed upon you as well." Joan put her hand on his. "I know you and I would help you in any way I can, but until then God seems disposed to bless us with a brood of children and I must look after your heirs."

"You always know what to say." He kissed her forehead.

That had been the last conversation they had before he went off to London, pretending to look sad to leave. He knew how much she regretted missing out on the royal marriage and had a small silver bracelet sent to her.

Another contraction hit her, this time more powerful than the last. She had to clench at the arm of a maid.

Was Roger dancing now? Was he feasting on sugar cakes and mulled wine?

Joan was getting remorseful the more she thought of the pain she had to endure while he had all the pleasure in the world.

It went on like this for nearly two days before a second son was born. Joan felt the long duration was punishment for ill-wishing her husband during her labor. Since the weather would prevent her from getting word to him, she decided to call the baby Roger to atone for her sins. Perhaps soon they would have a brood of children large enough that everyone in the family would have a namesake.

Exhausted, she had shortly collapsed into a slumber for almost two days. The midwives had managed to wake her only to drink broth at the urging of her worried mother-in-law.

On the third, she cradled her new son and introduced him to the rest of her children. Edmund himself was still just a babe, but Maggie pouted at the sight of him.

"He cries too much," she complained.

"You cried too," Joan tried to tell her, but Maggie wouldn't have anything to do with her youngest brother and asked to be excused back to her rooms in the nursery, where her nurse doted on her.

"She reminds me of my sister Maud," Joan told Margaret after her daughter had left. "A mean jealous streak runs through her." The baby cooed at the sound of her voice and it interrupted her grim thoughts.

"She is a child. We will teach her right from wrong," her mother-in-law replied with confidence.

"I know now how my mother must have worried over us. How you must have worried over how your own children would turn out."

"I still do." Margaret grinned. "Enjoy them while they are like this, soft and innocent." She touched the babe, feeling the soft black tuft of hair under her fingers.

∼

Roger finally rode home a few weeks later. In an attempt to keep the castle warm, Joan had all the fireplaces burning night and day. It was an extravagance that she would have to deal with later.

After he had seen the baby and pulled Joan into her bedchamber, he began telling her all that had happened.

"Queen Isabella is the perfect princess, and she comported herself with dignity."

"I cannot imagine a twelve-year-old having dignity." Joan scoffed. "What does she look like?"

"She has fair skin and golden hair."

"So poetic of you." She kissed his cheek and he turned, looking at her with tenderness in his eyes.

"I have eyes only for you, my beautiful fruitful wife." He pulled her flush against him to prove his point. "It is merely how everyone at court describes her." He shrugged.

"The wedding was at Westminster Cathedral, and even in the cold the city turned out to greet their new queen. However, after, the king snubbed his new wife."

Joan gasped. "What did he do?"

"Patience." Roger took a gulp of watered-down wine before he revealed what had happened. "After the ceremony, when everyone retreated to the great hall for feasting, he sat with Gaveston and not his queen at dinner. She was abandoned on the dais. Her French cousins and ambassadors were furious, of course, but hid their displeasure well enough."

"That is quite shocking. What could he mean by doing such a thing on his wedding day?"

"It is not our place to question the king, dearest. I am sure she shall help him see the errors of his ways."

Joan nodded, though she knew that her husband and several others did in fact question what the king was doing, especially when it came to his relationship with Gaveston. They were a jealous lot, and whether the rumors were true or not, she would rather not have treasonous words spoken in her household.

"So tell me, what do the ladies wear at court now?"

"How should I know?" Roger waved her off. "I hardly paid attention to the gowns of ladies."

"You are quite useless," Joan teased as she got out of bed. "I shall check on the children before I retire for the night. It is good to have you home, my love."

Roger stretched out on her bed and yawned. "I am glad too. It makes me happy to see our family together like this. Tomorrow I shall have to make sure the rents have been collected properly and deal with any issues or concerns people on our land may have."

"You are a gracious lord." She wrapped a warm robe around herself and slipped out of the room.

∼

For all of his words, Roger was more of a charismatic leader than a practical one. He did not like looking over account books or studying the health of his lands. He preferred giving orders and speeches. His natural charisma commanded his men and drew loyalty from them, but he was not an intelligent strategist, despite what he liked to think of himself. She knew that when tomorrow came, it would be his mother and her that would be looking over the rents and dealing with the smaller matters.

She could never see him becoming a great commander. Immediately Joan scolded herself for such a faithless thought.

The next day, after she had finished with the steward and the account books, she decided to take a tour about the castle.

She had gone to the dairy and the tannery, and now she was in the stables.

Her gray dapple mare, Isolde, was still in perfect condition. Joan fed her some oats as she stroked the horse's mane. She wished she had been able to ride her more, for she had a pleasant gait and could keep pace with any of Roger's stallions.

He had given her the horse as a gift following Edmund's birth, but Joan had shortly fallen pregnant and was unable to make much use of her.

As she was brooding over this, she heard noises coming from an empty stall at the end of the stable.

Frowning, she went to examine and was quite shocked to find Simon in the arms of a serving wench.

She gasped loudly and interrupted them.

"Milady!" the girl squeaked, pulling down her skirts. In a second she had sprung to her feet. Bowing deeply, she apologized again and ran off before Joan could say a word.

Simon was angrily trying to fix his trousers and had no sense to be embarrassed to be caught in such an act of sinfulness.

"I cannot have you harassing my maids," Joan coughed out. "I shall report this untoward behavior to my husband. I will not have my house become known for such behavior." Her voice was now angry at the thought of how this would seem to others. People would whisper that she could not manage her household and let her servants run around rutting like animals in the stables. She would not and could not condone such behavior.

Simon glared at her for a moment then schooled his features to appear undisturbed. "I'm sure your husband will not be surprised and would likely scold you for interrupting rather than lecture me." His voice carried the same biting anger toward her that her own had.

They did not like each other—that much was clear. Simon was at once both jealous and faithful to his master but hated his mistress with her airs. Being in his lord's favor, he was not scared of speaking to her with such frankness.

"Knave! Get out of here before I have you whipped."

He gave her a mock bow and ran out of the stables.

Joan frowned as she watched him disappear. She made a

mental note to speak to Roger about him. Simon was a terrible influence on all the other serfs, and now she had even more proof. Of course, Roger cared deeply for his childhood friend and had given him much more consideration than he deserved, at least in her opinion.

Perhaps it was her fear that he would rub off on Roger and that her husband would become like him. Letting anger and lust rule his decisions.

Joan would never let that happen.

It was night before she had the chance to speak to Roger. The babe had been giving the nursemaids trouble and Maggie, who was greatly upset, had hidden somewhere in the castle.

Usually, Joan would not trouble herself over such small matters, but it seemed to her as though everything around her was unraveling in disarray and she hastened to put everything right.

Roger would not share her bed until she was churched, but they sat together before the fire sharing a glass of wine.

"How was the hunt today?" She played with the corner of the napkin.

"Quite disappointing. I hope there hasn't been poaching on the land." Roger frowned.

"My lord, it is midwinter. I'm sure the beasts have hidden away. You don't need to blame the serfs for the rotten luck. I'm sure you shall fare better another day." Joan pacified him before he got it into his head that others were to blame for his own failure.

"Of course you are right, Joan." He sighed with a heavy heart. "It is just this blasted weather that has soured my mood. I shall hope for spring."

Joan did not respond for a while, but she knew something else was bothering him as well. He missed London. That much was clear. His mood had slowly deteriorated since arriving back home. She thrived in the respectable marshlands with their wilderness and freedom. In London, there was naught but gossip and fearful competition. At least here she was mistress.

Leaning over, she clutched his hand. "You shall be happy again, my love. Perhaps I shall order some minstrel to come and play a jolly tune for us."

"That's all right." Roger sighed again. "This melancholy shall pass. I will read in my room tonight."

He kissed her forehead to bid her goodnight.

"Wait!" she cried out before he could leave. "I was not sure if I would speak to you of this tonight, but that Simon of yours has been up to no good lately. Won't you see if you can speak to him? He tries my patience with his insults and his behavior toward me."

Roger's face darkened at that. "I shall, first thing tomorrow. Fear not, my lady."

Joan smiled at him in gratitude.

She said her prayers at her little prie-dieu and slipped under the warm furs that protected her from the winter chill outside.

The next day she was sewing shirts for Roger with Lady Margaret and some of their ladies sitting around them.

She had dreamt of Ireland that night, and it made her pang for it. Perhaps soon she would visit.

She heard shouts and screams outside and went to investigate. Joan was shocked by what she saw.

Roger was before Simon, who bowed at his feet. They were laughing and joking around together. She frowned from her window in the tower. She would ask Roger what he meant by this. He was supposed to have chastised the man, not celebrated with him.

When she found Roger in the great hall, he was with his squires and men-at-arms, drinking heavily. At the sight of the

Lady Mortimer with her hands on her hips and a fierce look in her eyes, they quieted.

"My lord, may I have a word with you in private?" The coldness in her usually soft voice shocked him, and he jumped to his feet to obey.

When they were in the hall, she demanded to know what he had said to Simon.

"Is this what this fury is about? I say, Joan, you should confess to the priest these sins of yours." He stroked the stubble on his chin.

"Tell me." She pressed.

"I have given him the commission to act as my steward and bailiff in Caedewen, Wales. He will be out of your way and banished to the north without giving offense to anyone."

"You reward him?!"

"No! Listen, Joan, I know you do not like him, but he is my friend and a good man. This will solve all your problems. I thought you would be pleased." Now Roger frowned at her, noting her blazing green eyes, and thought that wives should behave more calmly, like those in the folk tales and ballads.

Joan softened and retreated. "I do not trust him. He is too jealous and unhappy with his lot in life to be trusted with such responsibility. But I see the wisdom in your actions, and I thank you for your kindness to me."

He was pleased she had cleaved to him. "I do know what is best for our family. Trust me."

"I do, my lord." She curtsied to him and excused herself.

Upstairs, the ladies noted her silent fuming anger. She jabbed the needle through the cloth with a renewed vigor they had not seen in Lady Joan before.

Joan, for her part, was ignorant that she was drawing stares. All she could think of was how foolish Roger was. After all, had she not given him three children and looked after his lands with such care? He was greatly offended every time she disagreed with him, and she had to carefully mollify him.

Perhaps when he was older he would be wiser. But for now Joan longed to maintain their peaceful coexistence and his loving affection.

~

By early spring, Simon was all but forgotten. Joan had been churched and now spent much of her time with Roger, riding out on hunts with him, entertaining him with rowing competitions, and organizing masque. None of these entertainments were as grand as what they had in London, but Roger seemed pleased enough.

It was while Joan was exercising her gray mare that she saw a rider with her grandfather's livery come riding to the gates of the castle. She dug her heels into the horse's flank and shot forward at a canter.

She sighed with relief when she noted that his clothes were not trimmed with black, and therefore it could not be that her grandfather had passed away.

She crossed herself in thanks and slid off her horse before a groomsman could help her down.

"What news from Trim do you have for me?" she called out to him.

He turned immediately, identifying the Lady Joan Mortimer, and bowed. "It is a message from Lord de Geneville. He bids you and your husband come to Ireland."

"Is there trouble?"

"No, my lady." He smiled reassuringly. "He wishes to retire from his duties but wishes to see you one last time and make sure the lands are well looked after. He wrote a letter for you." He handed her the sealed letter.

"You are very welcome to Wigmore Castle. Tell my

steward who you are and he shall see you are properly housed. I shall speak to my husband immediately."

Rushing up the stairs to Roger's rooms, she flung the door open to his office without delay.

Roger jumped in surprise, his hand instinctively reaching for the dagger at his side that was not there.

"Happy news!" Joan cried before noting his expression. "Oh, I'm sorry, I did not mean to storm in here like that. But, Roger, I have such happy news."

"What is it?" Roger came to join her.

"My grandfather is planning to retire and leaves Castle Trim and all its responsibilities to us. Do you know what this means? We are coming into our own, and parliament will surely name you Lord Protector of Ireland!"

"My God, Joan!" He put his hands around her shoulders. "Say it again."

She laughed and repeated herself.

He joined her in her frivolity.

"I shall sail for Ireland as soon as possible," he declared once the excitement had died down.

"I shall come too."

"But the children." His brows scrunched in concern.

"Your mother can handle them. Besides, my grandfather would wish to see me. Please take me with you, for I do not wish to be parted from you." Her green eyes were wide and her lips pouted. Roger found he could not resist his pretty wife and kissed her sorrowful lips.

Finally, he whispered, "Of course you shall come if you wish it. We shall make arrangements. Now give me a smile."

He did not need to ask, for all of a sudden Joan was beaming up at him.

It was nearly a month before they could set sail. The messenger had been sent back to Ireland to tell his lord they were on the way.

Maggie, who continued to be sulky, was promised that she would travel with her parents to Ludlow, where she would be kept under the tutelage of Joan's mother Jeanne, who was feeling quite lonely as of late. Joan hoped that receiving special attention would soothe the child of her troubles.

On their way to Ludlow, Joan did not ride on a litter but rather side by side with her lord.

They made a graceful pair, Master Banner thought to himself. He was riding a mule not far from them and watched as they laughed and teased together. He could not help but feel that such happiness would be followed by equal sadness. There was a balance to life that had to be maintained. The wheel of fortune spun constantly, but he would pray that his mistress, who he had come to care for, would not be victim to its machinations.

The large retinue that followed them to Ireland did not include Simon, much to Joan's delight, and she hoped that she would no longer have cause to argue with her husband.

Maggie rode pillion behind them with Roger's bailiff. Being only five years old, she could not ride on her own, but she had tried to insist that she should get her own pony.

Roger had laughed at his daughter's demands and found them endearing. Meanwhile, Joan had frowned at what she saw as willful behavior not appropriate for her daughter.

They arrived at Ludlow and were welcomed with all the pomp one might expect.

Joan was greeted by her mother with increasing amounts of warmth. It seemed as she aged she clung more and more to family, where once she had been content ignoring them.

"How are you doing, Mother?" Joan inquired as they sat in her mother's solar. When Joan had first come in here, she had

JOAN

been surprised by how she was no longer blown away by the tapestries as she was when she had been a child. Compared to her own rooms, which had even grander tapestries and decorations strewn around them, Ludlow was starting to show its age.

"I am well, glad to have some company after so many years." Jeanne smiled softly. Managing the land no longer gave her the joy it once did.

"I shall have to give you an allowance to improve Ludlow some more." Joan decided. "It seems to have aged a bit since I last saw it."

Jeanne frowned. "It was not from lack of management or funds that I have not done much around the place. I simply wished to be thrifty with your inheritance."

"I did not mean anything by it. I want you to live in comfort and to have the house be the envy of all the county. This was my childhood home. I love it." Jeanne seemed comforted by that.

"New paneling for the great hall might be a good idea. We could get the carpenter to carve the Mortimer crest into it as well."

"Splendid suggestion." Joan turned to other thoughts. "You may find Maggie to be a handful. The nurses say she is going through a stage of jealousy and anger, but I wish to break her of such habits."

"I know how to deal with a spirited young lady." Jeanne grinned. "I'll whip her into shape."

"No doubt." Joan laughed but knew it was just as likely her daughter would be spoiled.

"Will you visit your sisters?" Jeanne broached the subject carefully. She knew they had written to each other very little and seen each other even less. It was not seemly for sisters to be so divided. Family was everything in this world.

Joan looked away as if to study the mantelpiece.

Out of resentment of her sister Maud and guilt over Beatrice, she had distanced herself from them. She felt responsible for the fact they were sent away to a convent against their will, even though Beatrice thrived in the religious life. Joan thought of Roger's own brothers and sisters, most of whom had chosen to leave the secular life and take up orders in various monasteries. Though she had originally accused Margaret of pushing her children to take up orders, she knew it was not so now. They had a true vocation.

"Perhaps." Joan bit her bottom lip.

"I know it makes you uncomfortable, but I am sure your sisters will be delighted in seeing you. It must be three years since you met face-to-face."

That night when Joan climbed into bed beside her husband, she told him of her mother's request with a heavy heart.

"It would be right for you to do so. Why are you so downcast?" Roger inquired.

"No reason really. Just a feeling I have."

Roger did not like seeing her so sad and sought to find a way to make her smile again. "Shall I massage your back?"

Joan blinked and then accepted his offer.

After she had relaxed, she pulled him close to her and they found themselves entwined together until morning.

Seeing how late in the morning it was, Roger smacked Joan's backside lightly. "Look here, woman. You kept me in bed until noon."

Joan squealed and threw a pillow at him. All decorum was lost with the pair, and this morning they were like newlyweds again.

"I shall have to go to the stockyard and see to our horses and supplies. The ship shall be ready to leave within three days, so you should see your sisters before then. Take Maggie if you wish." He kissed her again and called for his manservant.

She was not so eager to get out of bed. There would be little for her to do here anyway, for her mother ran the place with clockwork efficiency. Lying back on her soft pillows, Joan's thoughts once more turned back to her sisters. Maud would be twenty by now and Beatrice nineteen. These were no longer children but grown women. She did not need to fear them as she did.

The sun was high in the sky before Joan, freshly bathed and dressed in a gown of russet brown, joined her mother and daughter, who were playing in the rose garden.

"Mama!" The little girl leapt into Joan's arms when she noticed her. "Where were you? Grand-mère said you were taken by goblins."

"I'm here, sweetie." Joan tapped her nose. "I was merely tired. Have you been behaving?"

"Yes." Maggie nodded furiously. It was true that once away from Wigmore she had been on her best behavior.

"Well, I'm glad I won't have to lock you up." Joan set her back down on the ground.

"Good morning, Mother." Joan sat down beside her mother, who reproached her for staying in bed so late.

"I hope you are more productive at Wigmore Castle than you are here."

At once Joan felt like a child again with her mother's disapproving stare upon her. Would her mother never be pleased?

She had wanted to tell her that she had resolved to visit her sisters, but she decided to keep that to herself. She did not want to seem as though she could still be bossed around.

"Where is Roger?" She smoothed the skirt of her gown out around her.

"No doubt he went off with his men. He might be out hunting." Jeanne shrugged. She did not concern herself much with her young son-in-law.

"I heard the king will be going on summer progress with his new queen. I shall be sorry to miss the chance to see them."

"You shall be kept busy in Ireland no doubt." Jeanne herself was excited to see them. She had not taken the risk of traveling to London in the height of winter like Roger had and had not seen Isabella, who already had a reputation for being beautiful.

The trio passed the day languishing in the gardens around the castle. The maids brought them food and drink as they told stories and even sang songs together with little Maggie, who was keen to show them all the songs she had learned.

∼

The next day, Isolde had been saddled and was waiting beside a squire in the courtyard. Lady Joan had awoken early today to ride to Aconbury Priory. Out of childish spite she had not told her mother but informed Roger and Master Banner.

There was still dew on the grass as they rode out in the cool morning air. Joan relished this freedom and outpaced the squire on his old horse easily.

"Milady! Wait for me!" he had cried after her as he tried to urge his horse to go faster.

Eventually, she did slow to a leisurely pace and apologized to the man.

They met with very few travellers. Most people were in the fields tilling the soil and planting this year's harvest. They had little thought for anything else.

Joan stopped at an inn to feed the horses and eat something herself. "We don't have much longer to go," she informed Squire Edwin, who seemed anxious to get back on the road.

"As you say, milady." He had already finished his bread and roasted meat and wished to be gone from this place.

JOAN

Edwin was not one to disobey his lord, but he wished he had been given a better task than escorting the lady to an abbey. Lord Mortimer had been making plans to have a makeshift joust on the ground of Ludlow today, and he wished he could have participated.

The pair resumed their journey, though as they drew near, Joan was increasingly anxious.

The abbey seemed to materialize out of nowhere and she cringed, realizing she would have to face her fears.

A nun greeted them as they approached. She smiled kindly at them, noting their rich clothes and mounts.

"Good day, I am here to see my sisters, Maud and Beatrice, if they are available. I am Lady Mortimer." Joan introduced herself quickly. "This is my squire, Edwin."

"Yes, yes. If you will follow me, I shall see what I can do for you," the nun responded. "But I would wish that Master Edwin remain in the stable. I will send him food and wine."

"That sounds reasonable." Joan shot Edwin a side-glance and saw that he had bowed his head in acceptance.

The nun motioned for her to follow after her. Joan studied her black veil and black habit. She wondered if the nun wore a hair shirt underneath and shuddered at the thought.

Having deposited Lady Mortimer in a private room, the nun ran off to find Beatrice and Maud.

Joan waited for her sisters to come. She knew she had not followed precedent and sent a message ahead of her, but she was not planning to stay the night and saw no harm in dropping by unannounced.

Finally, the door opened and in stepped Beatrice. She was wearing the same black veil and habit that the other nun had been wearing, but it seemed to suit the pale creature. Joan noted that Beatrice was still small in stature and her pale face against the darkness of her clothes made her seem almost marble-like.

"Sister Beatrice, I am sorry to have stopped in so unannounced." Joan apologized after the two of them had greeted each other more formally.

"It does not trouble me." Beatrice's voice was light and airy. It no longer held the shy uneasiness that it had when she was a child. "You will have missed Maud though. She went to town with Sister Emily to tend to the sick and fetch the new novices."

"Ah, well I am sorry for that." Joan clasped her hands in front of her awkwardly.

"Shall we sit?" Beatrice smiled, guessing her thoughts. "I would love it if you told me of your family. How is Mother? She has not visited since last fall."

Joan jumped into telling her all the news. How baby Roger was thriving and all the quirks of the children and their adventures. She also told her of King Edward II's coronation and how grand the ceremony was.

Beatrice listened intently until it was her turn to tell all that had happened to her. "I took my vows last summer. Maud still has not." Beatrice frowned as she said that. "I have my lessons in botany and I help with the animals. Though the sisters do not like me chasing after chickens, as it is not befitting my station." She whispered the last part mischievously. "But I tell them God has called me to this work, and they cannot say much but scowl at me."

Joan laughed. "I am glad to hear you are enjoying your time here."

"You needn't feel guilty."

Joan gasped, for her sister had read her thoughts.

"We all must have our place, and I am lucky enough to be able to serve God in everything. You have a tougher life ahead of yourself than I do, Joan. Fear not for me but for yourself."

Joan gulped. Was this a premonition that her sister had?

The conversation turned to lighter topics after that.

JOAN

Beatrice was not interested in the outside world but listened to tales of Joan's children with an amused smile. In return, she told her sister of tales she had heard from travelers that had taken shelter here. She told her tales about the nuns and the pranks she had played with the other novices.

As the church bells rang announcing the turning of yet another hour and for the nuns to come to vespers, Beatrice had to excuse herself.

"It was wonderful seeing you again, sister." She kissed Joan's cheeks "Write to me."

"I promise I shall." Joan rode away from the abbey with a full heart. She was glad she had come and made peace with Beatrice, or at least she felt that she had been set free of the guilt she carried all these years.

On the way back she set a much calmer pace and even conversed with Edwin pleasantly, for she knew he was displeased at his charge and wished to keep him entertained.

They sang a jolly tune together, the crisp spring air urging them onward, making them forget their tiredness.

"I see the spires of Ludlow," Joan shouted back to the squire.

"So it is." He squinted, barely making out the crenellations.

"Shall we race?"

"As you wish, milady."

With a cry, Joan spurred her horse forward. She was overcome with a need to see Roger, to be with her family again.

The pair galloped into the courtyard. It was dark out now and they had startled several servants.

"Milady, let me help you down." Edwin helped her slide off her horse.

"That was well done, Master Edwin." Joan was breathing heavily. "I believe that was a draw."

Edwin bowed his head.

"Have a good night." She retreated through the main gate, making sure to instruct the groomsman to look after Isolde.

Her mother and Roger were seated around the great table. They were on their third course already.

Roger greeted her with a smile, but his eyes told her that her mother was upset.

Joan took a seat beside Roger and helped herself to some chicken and meat pies.

"How was your day?" Joan inquired.

There was silence. Roger coughed at the tension in the room.

"Mother, really. I am a married woman now. Why are you upset?"

"I am upset at your pettiness. I hoped you had outgrown that."

Joan scoffed. "I did as you asked. Do you not want to hear my news?"

"No, you will excuse me. I am tired and shall retire early tonight." Jeanne pushed the chair back as she stood.

"Why are you being like this?" Joan forgot all decorum as she spoke.

Jeanne did not reply to her daughter's impudent question but left silently.

Joan was alone with Roger now. The joy she had felt at her homecoming had lessened somewhat.

"How was your day, my love?" she questioned, taking another bite of her food.

"Well enough." Roger raised his glass so the servants might refill it. "You should have told your mother where you had gone. You are no longer a child."

"Then don't treat me like one."

Roger grasped her thigh under the table and squeezed

gently. "I didn't mean it, precious. You know how your mother gets. I don't wish for you two to fight."

"I shall speak to her tomorrow. Don't trouble yourself over this. We shall set sail soon," she responded, her mind on Ireland.

Her mother was keen on punishing her with her silence, but finally on their last day at Ludlow the two women reached an accord.

Jeanne had to realize that her daughter had gained some independence from her, and Joan promised to be more respectful.

"I don't know why I wished to hurt you like I did," Joan admitted. "Sometimes I feel such anger within me that I am afraid of it."

"It is your cross to bear. Take care of yourself and your husband. I can see how impatient he is for fame." Jeanne took her daughter by the arm and led her away from the company of gathered men and women. "Your grandfather wrote to me. He does not seem to think the king will declare Roger Lord Protector in his stead. I know Lord Mortimer is set on this, but you must prepare him for the bad news."

Joan hissed. "Why? Is he not suited? Roger has fought in many skirmishes and served the king well."

Jeanne shrugged. "You know I know nothing of the machinations of the English court."

Sighing, Joan fiddled with her purse strings. "I shall break the news to him once we reach Ireland. I could just imagine him marching off to London if he found out now."

"Take care on the journey. I shall look after Maggie and send you news as often as I can."

Joan kissed her mother's cold cheek and bid her farewell.

Within the hour, their party was back on the road, but Joan carried a heavy heart.

Joan found that despite his original misgivings, Edwin had

become her travel companion. Roger was increasingly distracted, and she looked to Edwin to amuse her on the journey. He was well versed in ballads and poetry, as had become popular at court as of late, and they played at cards in the evenings while Roger wrote his letters.

They reached port in a timely manner and boarded the hired ship. Joan was uneasy as she watched Roger pace about the bow of the ship. She carried a secret that she did not yet wish to divulge, so she avoided his company and spent more time with Edwin and her ladies.

Of her ladies, Jane Woods had become her favorite. They were both similar in age and disposition. Jane had come to serve her after her merchant father departed on a sea voyage to Italy. The daughter of a merchant was perhaps not the ideal companion for a baroness, but Joan found she did not care. Besides, Jane could tell her of the most fantastical places her father had visited and was better dressed than any of her other ladies.

She knew it was Mr. Woods's hope that she would find a fine husband traveling with Lady Joan. He dreamed of a knight for his daughter, though there was little chance of that happening.

Jane was quite impartial on the matter; she had not met any agreeable man yet and her father had been kind to her. He had not pressed her into an arranged marriage. Now, at nineteen, Jane was not quite so young anymore, and it was becoming more urgent that she wed.

Joan had not concerned herself greatly over this, for she knew her friend would tell her if she had her heart set on someone. Now on the boat ride to Ireland, she wondered if young Edwin, who was just twenty himself, though a squire, would be a good match.

Edwin came from a small, impoverished noble family who had barely been able to afford his apprenticeship under her

JOAN

husband, so she knew Jane's dowry would be highly attractive. Besides, they were both interesting people and would do well together.

Joan bit her lip, unsure if she was ready to play the matchmaker.

∼

The ship rolled into port, carried in by slow waves.

Joan stood side by side with her husband and watched as the city materialized before her.

There had been fog, and the ship's captain had been worried they were just as likely to hit the rocks as the shoreline.

The retinue disembarked. A hired litter was procured for her ladies and she chose to ride Isolde, who had been stuffed into the bow of the ship and was anxious to be on land again.

As everything they brought with them, from clothes to hunting dogs to boxes of jewels, was loaded into wagons and the servants ran around making sure nothing was lost, Joan and Roger set out ahead of them.

They would have to reach Trim by nightfall, lest they have to stay at an inn.

It was hard going, for it had rained over the last few days and the roads were slick with mud. Those on horseback fared better than those in litters and wagons, which constantly got stuck in the mud.

Roger was already cursing at this wild country.

Joan wondered if he would be glad now that he would not be named Lord Protector, for he seemed to want to run back to the comforts of home.

"When the sun is shining you shall come to love Ireland as I do, husband," Joan promised him.

Roger looked at her with skepticism, but he did not

disagree with her. She had been right several times before and he knew he tended to be impatient.

Trim Castle's gray walls provided a depressing sight. Among the fog that still clung to the earth and the dark sky, it looked haunted by ghosts and abandoned.

Of course, it was not. At the sound of their horses, several guardsmen came to investigate who had approached. Seeing Roger's and Joan's emblems, they bowed low and called inside the bailey for serfs to help the arriving party.

Joan hopped down and led Roger inside. She had stayed here a month years ago, but she remembered the way to the great hall.

Her grandfather was not there as he had always been, and his steward said he had retired early from an ache in his bones.

"He will be happy to see the both of you." The man spoke with a heavy Irish accent. "He has been mighty lonely ever since Lady Matilda passed away."

"I can only imagine. Please, show us to our rooms, good sir, for we are weary from our journey." Joan stifled a yawn.

Roger complained of the dampness in their room, but Joan poked him and said he was acting like a spoiled child and that his complaints were all in his head.

In truth, the next day they both awoke in better spirits. The sun was shining overhead and the fog had dissipated.

Joan took Roger onto the parapet and they stared out at the rolling green hills of the countryside as the sun began rising.

"It shines like fields of emeralds from a distance," Roger commented, staring transfixed upon the land. "I see now why you dreamt of returning here." He kissed her cheek.

They stood there for a few more moments before Joan pulled him away. "Let us go and greet my grandfather."

When they entered his private dining room, Joan had to hold back a gasp. Her tall imposing figure of a grandfather had been replaced with a haggard old man. All that remained of the man she once knew was his shining dark eyes that still sparkled with intelligence.

"Ah, Joan, so you've come at last." He coughed, holding out a hand for her.

She rushed forward and kissed it tenderly. "My lord, you are ill."

"It has been a long time. I have merely aged." Geoffrey paused and looked up at Roger, who was standing nearby. "I assume that is your husband."

"Yes. Baron de Geneville, please meet Lord Roger Mortimer."

Roger stepped forward and bowed low, showing him great respect.

Geoffrey in turn tipped his head to him. "I cannot get up very well these days, so you will excuse me for remaining seated. Please help yourselves to some food." He pointed to the table behind him, which held several plates of smoked meat and eggs as well as other foodstuffs.

As they ate and a servant helped Geoffrey sip down his ale, he questioned the pair.

While his body was failing him, Geoffrey still had his mental capacities, although he was slower at expressing himself.

This winter had been tough on him and he could no longer deny that he would not be able to continue his duties for much longer. He wished to see the transfer of power go smoothly. The Irish were wary of strangers, and Geoffrey wished to ensure his heirs were well established before he left.

They talked well into the afternoon. Besides pleasantries and news of the family, they spoke of management of the land and plans Roger had.

After their conversation, Geoffrey bid Joan sit with him by the fire, dismissing her husband.

"He seems like a decent young man. He is ambitious and sure of himself."

Joan nodded in agreement.

"Parliament has written to me. They will not make Roger Lord Protector, at least not yet."

"I have guessed as much. Mother mentioned something to me before I left."

"I hope he will take the news well." Geoffrey scratched his snowy white beard. "There's something else. I will speak to Roger of this as well, but you will be left with many enemies in taking up these holdings of mine. I fear I shall retire to peace and comfort and leave you to deal with the mess." Then he reached over and patted her as if she was a child once more. "You are a smart girl."

"A woman now, Grand-père," Joan reminded him with a soft smile. "We will take good care of the lands you have entrusted to us. Have no fear."

"Yes, yes. Now off you go." He sent her off.

In truth, he had been told of rumors that King Robert the Bruce had his eyes set on Ireland for his younger brother, Edward. Of course, these were rumors, but that was not all. His deceased wife's family, the De Lacys, had also been causing trouble in parliament back in England. They had no love for de Geneville, and worse than that they were seeking to make ties with the Scots. Geoffrey feared what this would mean for his granddaughter, but she seemed settled and had already borne three heirs for the family. Her husband too was no fool, which was a boon to the family.

Geoffrey would have to tell them about all of these rumors. To be forewarned was to be prepared.

Joan and Roger spent half the year in Ireland, and after establishing themselves and leaving loyal servants to manage their estates, they returned back home. This would be a yearly trip and perhaps a more permanent home if Roger would be named to his position.

When Roger heard the king had not wished to pass on the title of Lord Protector to him, he had fumed. This was a boy who had been raised to be handed everything he wanted. He felt he had done his duty and wished to be rewarded. Joan had finally managed to pull him out of sulkiness when she told him she was expecting a child once again.

With her grandfather installed at the House of the Friars Preachers, they hastened back to England while it was still safe to travel.

A third son, Geoffrey, was born at Ludlow that Christmas.

CHAPTER 8

1315-1316

"Come back here!" Joan lifted her skirts so she could run after her rapscallion children.

Roger had gone hunting with his men, and in an effort to join them in the fun, Joan had brought her children and made a makeshift picnic outside the boundaries of the forest. Only Jane, her lady in waiting, and two nursemaids had accompanied them.

Jane had indeed married Squire Edwin, after their parents came to a suitable agreement. They lived together serving the Lord and Lady Mortimer. Joan had patted herself on the back for making such a fine match.

Currently, she was chasing after Margaret, Edmund, and Roger, who were running away from her, calling her a witch.

Their fun and games were not usual for the family, who at all times had to observe some sort of decorum.

The squeals of her eldest children's laughter filled Joan with glee.

They should do this more often.

Eventually, she caught up to them and scooped Roger and

Margaret into her arms. Edmund, who was the smartest of the bunch, had climbed up a tree out of reach.

"I'm going to eat you, naughty children." Joan teased, tickling the pair of them.

Edmund, finding his bravery, called out, "Nay! You cannot, for I will stop you."

"From all the way up there?" Joan laughed. "I shall like to see you try."

Picking up her prisoners again, she began jogging back to the blankets and tables set up for their amusement.

"I shall race you back, and if you win I shall not eat them."

Margaret, now thirteen but still small, tried to shake loose, but after dealing with all her children for these many years, Joan knew how to hold tight to them.

In the end, Edmund, who was not encumbered by anyone, managed to beat her back.

As promised, she released his siblings.

"You weren't really going to eat us, were you, Mother?" Roger, who was only nine years old, asked.

"No, you are much too thin. Go eat some mutton. I want to fatten you up." Joan ruffled his hair and thought wistfully that soon both her eldest boys would be sent off together to squire for her husband's uncle, Roger de Chirk. At least she would not be lonely.

After Geoffrey had joined her ever growing brood, John and Katherine had joined the nursery as well. They were still babes, barely able to walk themselves, but Joan enjoyed their company whenever she could. She knew that soon they would be returning to Ireland for a prolonged stay. While she and Roger went back every year for a few months or so to look after Trim and make sure everything was running smoothly, she knew that this year would be different.

The rumors that the Bruce family of Scotland had their eye on Ireland had been realized. The king's brother, wishing for a crown of his own, had promised the people to bring back their old Gaelic ways and be a true King of Ireland. Worse yet, the De Lacys were rumored to be supporting him.

Roger would no doubt be called to stop any rebellion and crush the usurper. Joan had already determined she would accompany her husband to war if it came to that. In their years together she had come to love him deeply. They were friends confiding in each other but also lovers. Their children were proof enough of that. God seemed to smile on them.

Little John, who was five now, crawled over to her and pulled at her skirt for her attention.

"What is it, little one?"

He fluttered his blonde eyelashes at her and stretched his hands out to her to be picked up.

Of all her children it was John who resembled his father the most, but he was quiet and seemed content to play the babe, even though Joan knew full well that he could walk and talk.

"What shall I do with you, my spoiled little lord?" She winked at him as she picked him up.

Immediately, she regretted bending over as she had, for a pain shot up her side and she couldn't help but call out.

Jane was by her side immediately. "Is it the babe?" she whispered. Her mistress was on her seventh pregnancy, and while she had been lucky and only had one miscarriage the year before, she wondered how long her luck would last. Joan was thirty now and was no longer so young that she could recover right after each pregnancy. It was only her active spirit that seemed to bring her back each time.

"It is all right. I have pushed myself too much today. Sometimes I forget my condition." Joan brushed her off with a soft laugh. "My lord husband should be returning soon." She peered up at the sky, noting the sun was beginning to set. "Perhaps we should pack up what we can so we may return back to the house once the hunting party arrives."

Jane nodded and set about instructing the nursemaids to help while Joan sat down to rest. Margaret, who was now much calmer as she grew and no longer resented her mother as she once had, approached her tentatively.

"Can I help you with anything?"

"No, dearest. But do keep an eye on Katherine. She loves escaping from us ever since she has learned to walk. Only my daughters seem to give me trouble." Joan shook her head as if in weariness, but Margaret knew she was not serious.

She departed to go fetch Katherine, who was waddling away toward the forest as her mother had predicted, since the nursemaids were distracted.

"Katie, don't be so naughty." Margaret picked her up in a swoop and returned to her mother's side. The rest of her brothers and sisters had gathered around her and were listening with great interest as she spoke of Ireland and the great adventures Joan had while she was there last.

"Your father and I were hunting in the woods when all of a sudden there came a mighty roar to the side of us." Joan paused for effect. The boys were entranced but also quaking with fear. They had heard the tale many a time, but it was still as fresh and new as ever. "I could not see. The wind had whipped my veil into my face, but it was just as well. Your father gave a great shout and said to rush back. I quickly obeyed, digging my heels into my horse's flank, and on we rode. When we caught up with the rest of the camp there were great shouts and a flurry of arrows. Finally, I turned around and saw from my saddle a huge black beast with fierce red eyes."

"The bear!" shouted Geoffrey.

"Yes, the bear. It was almost upon me, but your father brandished his sword and, turning, faced the beast head-on.

He swung with a strength that surprised everyone and the bear fell silent and was dead."

"Hooray!" shouted the boys.

Joan laughed with them. The story was true enough. Of course, she had embellished the tale somewhat. The bear had not been that close to her, and it was half dead from being struck by arrows before Roger had put it out of its misery.

～

It was not long before Roger and the hunting party returned. Joan watched Thomas Berkeley with a special interest. Roger and Maurice, the Baron of Berkeley, were in talks to arrange the marriage between his eldest son Thomas and her eldest daughter Maggie, who was now nearly ready to be married herself. Thomas was a handsome enough fellow; he was not so old yet either. Maggie would not have to balk at marrying an old man and he came from a distinguished family, so she would be kept in the same luxury she had been accustomed to.

Within a year or two her little princess would be married.

Joan shook her head. Had so much time really passed? She had been married for nearly fifteen years.

Standing up, Joan greeted her husband joyously, hiding her own discomfort, and he swung down from his horse, urging the party to return to the castle with their catch so he might walk back with his children and wife.

Roger offered Joan his hand, which she took gladly. He studied his wife with an increasing awareness of her fragility. While she had certainly grown plumper after all her pregnancies, she had maintained her figure as best she could, and while there was the hint of wrinkles on her face, it still contained that same fiery spark from her early days. Roger gave thanks he still had a handsome wife while many were shackled to haggard plain women.

But now with the latest announcement of her pregnancy he had noted a change about her. She seemed to tire often and could not stomach any food. He worried this might be her undoing. He prayed every day that she would be healthy and return to him strong as ever. What would he do without her?

As they walked, Joan had no inkling of her husband's thoughts. Her mind was on the accounts once again and how they would manage this winter, for the crop had been bad and many of the sheep on their lands had fallen sick and died. It was a toll, but at least they had enough tucked away.

Roger's mother greeted the party at the gate with a firm look of disapproval.

Joan waved the aged woman's worries away.

"You must think of the babe and not go gallivanting around the countryside in your condition." Lady Margaret scolded her.

"I did not ride." Joan huffed. Thinking of riding almost brought her to tears, for it reminded her of Isolde. Her trusted mare had suffered a limp last spring and had never recovered. Joan refused to set her aside just yet and used the gentle mare to teach her younger children to ride about the small paddock built for her.

Wiping away her tears, she wondered what was making her so emotional. None of her other pregnancies had been so.

"Fret not. I did not wish to upset you so." The elder Margaret put a hand over her trembling one. "You should lie down."

Joan did not bother explaining that she had not cried because she was being scolded like a child. It was simply her pregnancy making her emotions run amok.

Several quiet months passed and her pregnancy progressed at an astonishing rate. Her belly grew bigger than it had ever done before, while Joan seemed to shrink away from not getting enough food. Of course, she noticed nothing of this, preferring to continue on as usual.

～

Then the king's herald showed up at Wigmore Castle.

Roger had yet to return to court, but now there seemed to be no need. He was to go to Ireland and muster up an army to defend it against Edward Bruce.

Joan crossed herself at the news. It had still seemed a distant possibility, but now her husband was to go off to war.

There was still plenty of time left before they would set sail, and this babe would be born by then. As she watched her husband prepare for battle, she dreamt of the lazy spring they had spent hunting and running around with their children. They had visited all their manors and brought the children to see her mother at Ludlow.

Now Edmund and Roger had been packed away to their uncle's house, and the rest of the children were sent to her mother to watch over them.

Joan was adamant that she would still go to Ireland with Roger.

The week before she was supposed to enter her confinement, her waters broke. The midwives came running from the village. Nothing was done right, but this babe would not wait.

After two days laboring, the household was shocked as two babes were welcomed into the world. Two little babes named Joan and Agnes.

Joan wept when she saw them. They were tiny to be sure, but they were strong and healthy. She prayed for a whole afternoon on her knees, thanking Mary for being merciful.

She had little time to enjoy her new babes, for they would set sail in three months, leaving them behind.

Roger had suggested she stay behind with them, but Joan

knew her place was by his side now that she was well enough to travel and had recovered greatly.

They were on board the ship staring out at the rolling ocean when Roger peered at her with a soft smile. "You look much better, sweetheart."

Joan looked up, for he had never called her that.

"You gave me quite a fright." He kissed her temple. "But I am glad to see you are looking so well. There's color in your cheeks again."

Joan rubbed them. "It's only because of this chill. I did not know you were frightened for me." She looked at her hands.

"Yes, we have quite a brood now. Perhaps it would be best if we take care."

Joan caught the meaning behind his words. They were blasphemous to be sure, but she understood where he was coming from and knew she should be grateful.

"As long as you keep me by your side." She leaned against him.

"I shall never send you away." Her quiet innocent voice awakened the chivalric knight within him.

"Good."

∽

This journey to Ireland was different from the other they had taken. They were not going to Trim Castle through Ludlow. Instead, their ship, filled with Roger's men, landed north and they marched through the countryside, visiting with local leaders to ensure their loyalty and garner their support.

It was a show of strength and it worked...until in the spring of 1316 Edward Bruce with his five thousand men arrived and began laying waste to the north.

"Violence will not tame the Irish to his will." Joan seethed when she heard the news. It was true she was an Englishwoman, but she had come to love Trim and all of its people. She held a special place in her heart for them.

"It is our loyal Irishmen he seeks to tame. One way or another he will have reached his goal. They will either bend the knee to him or die by his sword. He cares not." Roger shrugged.

This sort of brutality horrified Joan, whose images of war were molded by the stories she had read.

Victory did not come so quickly or easily as it did in stories.

They had received rumors that there was a plague in England and so reinforcements would not be so quick to arrive. King Edward II was more interested in his poetry and a new favorite, Hugh Despenser, than making war. Roger was quick to curse him these days. Luckily, he had only done so in her presence or that of Master Banner, who frowned but did not comment.

The downfall of Gaveston in 1311 had been swift. Even the king could not protect him from the angry Ordainers, a group of lords who demanded reforms, including the earls of Lancaster and Warwick. Initially, Gaveston had been exiled as per their request, but he returned not even a year later and the king revoked his exile. Of course, this did not sit well with the Ordainers. There were many skirmishes Joan had been aware of, but it ended with Warwick capturing Gaveston again and beheading him on Lancaster's lands.

It was a sorry business that had left the country in shambles. Now it seemed that it had all been for naught. The king had simply taken another favorite.

There was little for Joan to do while in Ireland. She made sure they had plenty of supplies if there was to be a siege, kept a steady stream of letters going between herself and their lands in England, and being a companion for her husband.

From her perspective there was no war save for the

warriors encamped in the castle, the reports they received, and the fact that her husband had taken to striding around in chainmail with a sword in his hilt.

Skirmishes were fought all up and down their lands. For the most part, Roger held his ground, but he was fearful that the Bruce was gaining a foothold. The north of Ireland, which he had marched his army through at first last spring, had fallen to him. He tried to keep this from Joan and, besides, there was nothing to worry about.

In the south, the Irish generals loyal to the crown were mustering a proper army to help push back the invading army, and in England, King Edward had promised more men and gold to pay for mercenaries.

Both Roger and Joan had to wait with bated breath, doing what they could until this real help finally materialized in November when they feared it was too late.

On an English warship arrived men, money, and a letter that surprised Roger. He was named Lord Lieutenant of Ireland and he was to push back the Scots.

With tears pouring down her face, Joan bid Roger farewell as he led his army to battle against the de Lacys and the Scots.

The Irish lords were armed and ready to march at his command as well.

Pushing her rosary into Roger's hand, she urged him to stay safe.

He made a great show of tying it around his wrist then drinking from the cup of wine she offered him before he shouted to his generals and they rode off.

Joan did not stay to watch them disappear. In her heart she knew that no matter what he had to come back, but she should prepare herself in the event he did not.

In the many days and nights that lay ahead of her, she thought little of battles and wished to hear of no news except that from England and if her husband said it was done.

She did not know what made her a coward, for she had never felt such a fear before. Perhaps it was something else she feared, the physical distance between herself and her husband, but that was silly, for they were often apart.

Regardless, she threw aside such thoughts by focusing on the task at hand.

Embroidering should not have been her chief concern at this time, but in this moment of weakness it distracted her and numbed her to the fact she was in a country at war and her husband was at this very moment engaged in a battle.

Two weeks had passed and there seemed to be a standstill for now. A winter storm had forced both armies into retreat and they were waiting for the weather to pass.

Another week went by and an impatient Joan had moved past fear. She needed to be doing something practical. Of course, she could not wield a sword, but surely there could be something.

The servants had balked at her pacing the great castle. They thought she was going quite mad.

Joan sent Jane to fetch the master of the horse. At length, he appeared before her. It was not out of discourtesy that he had taken so long, but he had to attend to the horses. New ones had arrived and he had to inspect them before sending them off to Baron Mortimer.

He bowed low before the white-faced lady.

"I wish to ride. Could you have a horse ready for me?" Joan asked impatiently.

"W-why, that is impossible. It is not safe. Surely your ladyship knows that." He balked, refusing to meet her gaze.

"I shall go. Not far, but I am tired of being cooped up here. It is driving me to madness."

He gulped when she said this.

"You will permit me to send a guard with you and to have

the master of arms send a scout first to make sure there is no danger?"

Joan sighed but agreed. Of course, this was sensible. "Send for me when the horse is ready," she commanded and waved the man off.

It was three long hours before she was able to go riding.

No risks were to be taken with the baroness. The master of the horse was sure his master would have his hide for letting her leave the protective castle walls.

She rode around the castle, cantering and only veering toward the fields slightly every now and again. In the bleak chilly afternoon, the silence outside the castle seemed eerie. A thin blanket of snow covered the ground and she thought it was best to not venture too far.

An hour later she was returning to the gatehouse, sensing her guard was getting increasingly worried the longer he was out here as well, when she heard the soft tread of horses approaching.

She hurried inside and ran up to the parapet to see who had come. Her fur cloak billowed around her as she squinted to see the riders.

There were three hooded men. Two flanking the middle man. Neither had banners nor anything that would give away who they were.

Joan's heart clenched.

Then as they approached the gate, before they were within the shot of arrows, the middle man threw back his hood, revealing Roger's gleaming face.

"Roger!" she called, unable to stop herself as she waved frantically.

Quickly, the drawbridge was lowered and he was allowed in.

He handed the reins to the waiting groomsmen and rushed to meet Joan as she ran down the steps.

"Victory! Victory!" he cried as he spun her around. Then, putting her back down, Roger turned to the gathering crowd. "We have pushed back Edward Bruce to Carrickfergus and the de Lacys into Connaught. The Earl of Louth will see to the rest."

There were cheers in the gathered crowd. It was nearing Christmas and this was just what they needed to hear.

Joan felt a weight lift off her chest as she turned to her husband. "Let me help you change into something more comfortable. Why did you come riding up like that?"

"This is war, Joan. I wanted to get here as soon as possible, but I could not let myself be so easily recognized."

Joan looked down. Of course, she should have realized that.

"Now come along." She pulled him along even as many people looked as though they wished to speak to him.

For a moment he is mine, she thought to herself. Then they can have him back.

She poured him a cup of mulled wine and sent for food to be brought to him, and as he ate he told her everything there was to know.

It seemed that Edward Bruce's policy was going to be his own undoing. He enjoyed razing manors to the ground and stealing all of the supplies from the local villages and lords. Those who had once joined and supported him willingly were starting to doubt their allegiances. He had made more enemies than friends, and he was having a hard time feeding his army.

Everyone was, though, Roger moaned. Joan knew that their crops had not been as plentiful as before, but she was horrified to learn that all over Europe this was the case. It seemed that this year's crop in Ireland would be just as bad, and it did not help that Bruce was burning the little crops that were thriving.

Joan felt a rise of shame inside of her. While she had been

preoccupied with her worries for her husband, she had not put much importance on the crops or the struggles of her people. She would rectify this immediately.

After he had finished eating, Joan put her hand over his. "Will you be strong enough to speak to the people downstairs? They looked anxious to hear the news from you before I stole you away."

"Yes, the food has helped me recover some of my energy, but make sure to steal me away before it gets too dark." He kissed her brow, making his implication clear, and Joan could not help but blush.

"As you wish, my lord."

CHAPTER 9

1318-1319

The consequence of that night of bliss became evident two months later when Joan noticed she had missed her courses. Far from being upset, she was filled with hope that this signaled a turn. Perhaps they would even be back in England before the babe was born.

As her belly grew week by week, Joan occupied herself with making careful provisions of the stores of food they had. She knew the people of their lands were struggling and tried to send them food from her own larders whenever she could. Roger had been angry when he had heard of this, but she reasoned with him that they needed to keep the people happy lest they rebel too or perish, leaving the land in the spring without any workers to plant new crops.

As it was, she was left to her own devices for the most part.

Roger was still being called away to deal with skirmishes and help put down rebels that kept rising up, but, for the most part, he was nearby and not gone for longer than a few weeks at a time. As Lord Lieutenant, he also had other duties including collecting taxes and hearing the complaints of the lords.

JOAN

It was decided by the king that Roger could be relaxed with taxes on those nobles that were loyal to the crown and who had provided men to the defense of Ireland. This proved to be a popular decision as it also increased the number of nobles willing to send their men to fight against the Bruce and his evil men.

～

That Christmas was a joyous one, even though Joan refused to have the customary feast Trim was used to holding. Besides, there was hardly anything extra in the larder that could be scraped together. Joan refused to enter her confinement until after the Christmas season.

She still had the hall decorated with holly and evergreen needles. The Yule log was made and filled the great hall with its delicious smell as it burned. In an effort to show Christmas charity, she sent many of her servants home with packages of food to make sure that their families had something to eat. She apologized for the meager offerings, but they seemed pleased nonetheless.

Everyone knew that there was famine everywhere and would not refuse any food. They themselves knew that their lords and ladies were hardly eating better than they were.

Thus, in the second week of January Isabelle was born. She would be another mouth to feed, but her mother did not fret over such things and took joy in her little smiles and innocent cooing. What did this babe know of hunger?

Unfortunately, they had not been able to return to England that year nor the next. The Bruce managed to hold on and still received support from his brother. Meanwhile, the Pope in Rome had not declared his cause illegitimate, but nor did he support him. The English and their Irish supporters would have to rid themselves of him.

Joan fell pregnant again in the winter of 1318.

She laughed at her own fertility. It was starting to be unseemly that at her age her husband was still visiting her bedchamber so often and that she had the indecency to fall pregnant so soon after her last baby. But she knew she was blessed and thanked God every time she went to mass.

In June, as Joan was tallying the good harvest they seemed to be having this year, she heard news from London that the queen had been delivered of a healthy baby girl named Eleanor. This was her third child, and England rejoiced that they now also had a princess.

Bad news followed soon after when a letter arrived from her mother at Ludlow. It was written in a shaking hand that Joan was unaccustomed to seeing.

As it turned out, her sister Maud had brought great shame upon the family. She was still a novice at the age of thirty, which was unheard of, but no one could make her take her vows. However, now she had run away with a weaver from the local village whom she had visited often. It was rumored they had run away to France. Jeanne told her daughter that she had immediately renounced her evil daughter and forbade Joan from trying to find or contact her as well.

Joan crossed herself. Of course, she had no great love for Maud and was horrified at her actions, but at the same time she understood in her heart that her sister, desperate for love, had found a way to escape the convent into which she had been forced.

She wondered what this meant for her sister Beatrice, who would now be directly stained by her sister's actions.

Would this ruin her own chances to rise higher in the church?

Roger had cheered her up by presenting her with a new

JOAN

mare. This one was a deep chestnut with kind dark eyes. She was excitable, unlike her gentle Isolde had been, but she was surefooted and a beauty in her own right. She had named this creature Marigold.

She had taken a turn about the castle with her despite her condition, and it put her in good spirits.

In the next moment, Roger announced the formal betrothal of their daughter Margaret to Thomas Berkeley. Their daughter Katherine was also to be married to a ward. However, Roger swore it would be many years before they would live together as man and wife, for they were both still so young. This had been a purely political decision, for he wished to keep the young Earl of Warwick's lands and fortunes in his family.

"When will the weddings take place?" Joan inquired anxiously at the news.

"Not until we get back to England, my sweet." He reassured his wife.

"That is good. I should not wish to miss our first child's wedding." She smiled and went off to write Margaret a letter asking her what she would like as a gift. She wished to ask her if she was happy with the arrangements but did not bother. It was a good match, and her daughter would have to resign herself to it even if she was unhappy.

She was nearly six months along when the harvest was being pulled in. The servants joked that their fertile mistress had blessed this year's harvest, for it seemed as though the famine had finally broken and they had managed to produce a fine yield.

Joan was so happy that they did not have to worry about this upcoming winter that she gave the servants a day off so that they might celebrate and rest after all their hard work.

Then to sweeten the mood even more, two months later they received news from Louth that at the Battle of Faughart,

Edward Bruce had fallen and his army had scattered or were destroyed.

Roger had balked when he had heard that the foolhardy Bruce had not waited for reinforcements but led his five thousand men to battle against an army that was rumored to be twenty thousand strong. No legendary Scottish strength could overcome such odds.

Still, this now meant that after two years of being away from their children they could finally return home.

～

They arrived at Ludlow with much fanfare. Her mother had arranged for a big celebration, even though it was not yet Christmas, and they feasted and dined there with their children. Only a few days later Joan had to enter her confinement at Ludlow. Already she had postponed doing so, but her mother had pointedly begun preparing her rooms and would brook no disagreement.

"You must take care of yourself. You are thirty-two now." Jeanne had shaken her head. In a way, she was jealous of her daughter and all the children she had given her husband. On the same hand, she was incredibly proud.

Roger had left soon after to give his report to the king and Ireland but promised he would bring her to court for the New Year's celebrations, should she be churched by then.

Joan kept Margaret, Katherine, and the twins, who were still toddlers, with her. Her sons, Geoffrey and John, had grown while she was gone and Roger had sent them to be page boys for the Earl of Hereford. All her sons had written to her that they were glad she had returned and could not wait to see her. They would be released from their duties and return to Castle Wigmore for Christmas.

Thoughts of this happy reunion kept Joan occupied until

JOAN

she went into labor in early November and delivered another little girl. This baby looked awfully pale and small. She was also worryingly quiet, but she thrived on her nursemaid's milk. Joan had thought about her name for a long time before settling on Beatrice. Perhaps her holy sister would protect this sickly babe.

As she recovered from the birth, Jeanne, who was much aged as of late, told her of the plague that had culled England's population significantly and the bad harvests.

"We shall have to pray that it does not come back for a couple more years." Joan agreed.

The family would have to be more tight-fisted with their money now. Not only did they have Margaret's dowry to contend with, but they had to recover the losses to their coffers.

Unexpectedly, Roger appeared at Ludlow. He had only been gone for a couple of weeks. His quiet seething anger confused Joan, but she was still too weak to concern herself too much over him.

He was often unruly and angered whenever he returned from court. It was a wonder why he ever went back there.

When they traveled back to Wigmore with their daughters, Joan decided it would be best to talk to him now. Otherwise, he would remain like this throughout the Christmas celebrations.

When they stopped to get fresh horses, Joan approached him.

"So, why do you carry that grimace?"

Roger remained silent for a long time before putting words to his fury. "The king is mad," he hissed. "We got rid of one favorite only to have another replace him. We all blamed Gaveston for his follies, but now I see he was blameless and it is the king's own nature to be fickle and hateful." He whispered these treasonous words even though they were alone, as the rest of their party was running around watching the wagons and eating some food to replenish their strength.

"My lord?" Joan gasped. She had not known his hatred ran so deep.

"Hugh Despenser the younger holds all of the king's favor now. His father had been loyal to him when the whole mess with Gaveston took place. King Edward showers them with rewards and ignores all others. I was not asked to stay for Christmas and was given a mere thanks for my contributions in Ireland."

"King Edward fought his own battles here. There are many war heroes to thank. Perhaps when the time comes he will reward you properly. You must forgive him. He is our sovereign."

Roger scoffed at that and Joan pressed forward.

"We have all we need, and while we are not in the highest of favor, at least we are not distrusted. So be careful that we do not lose the king's love, no matter how little we may have."

Roger pushed her hand off his shoulder. "I did not yet tell you the best part. He mentioned my lands in the north of Wales and asked whether I was sure I held them rightfully or if they had come to be in my possession by mistake!"

Joan gasped at that. "What did you say?"

"I told him that his father had given me my letters patent himself and they were rightfully mine. He merely waved me away and said he would look into the matter." Roger let out an exasperated sigh. "I tell you, Joan, I will not stand by if he seeks to take away my lands."

"No, you should not, but tread with care." She urged him still to be cautious, though she herself was now angered. Had their family not served the crown faithfully?

They rode on soon after their conversation. Roger seemed in better spirits now that he had told someone of his troubles, but he was not nearly soothed.

JOAN

He tried to think of something else and was surprised when the beautiful Isabella appeared unbidden into his mind. She had stood on her throne majestic and pale. Her golden hair shone under her veil, dulling the gold of her crown. He had been mystified. Roger shook his head. It was not right he thought of her like this.

∽

Wigmore Castle seemed to be overflowing with the return of Baron Mortimer and all of his ten children.

Lady Margaret, now a very old woman, was beside herself at the loud rambunctious children that were running amok. She had lived a tranquil existence prior to their arrival and she was quite taken aback.

Roger had apologized to his mother, but she waved his concerns away.

This was her cross to bear. She could rest in the next life.

When she heard this, Joan nearly laughed. The woman thought laughing children were a punishment sent to her by God. She shook her head at the prideful woman who could not see that this was no punishment, but a gift to her to see how successful her line would be.

Joan, for her part, marveled at how much her older children had grown. Her boys were slowly becoming men, and she wondered if she should start looking for a wife for her eldest as well. Edmund was eighteen and had done well as a squire under the Lord de Chirk. Roger had said he was sure he would be knighted soon enough.

They celebrated Christmas and New Year's together, and despite their father, who was still gloomy, the rest of the family contented themselves with dancing around the great hall and making merry.

Katherine and Margaret would be married before Easter

and then accompany their family to court for Easter. A royal summons had been sent shortly after New Year's, and Joan hoped this visit would go over better with Roger.

Katherine's wedding was merely a ceremonious affair, for both she and her groom were still children.

With the final contracts signed and sealed, Margaret was married out of Wigmore Abbey in March 1319.

The grim expression on her face went unnoticed by her bridegroom, who was grinning from ear to ear. He had admired Margaret and her fiery beauty for years. Margaret was impartial herself, but she was unhappy that she would be living at his manor home in Bristol. The thought that she would become a baroness like her mother seemed to placate her.

Joan watched as her daughter, decked in a gown of green satin, danced with her husband. She was graceful and would bring him much joy, she thought. She also hoped her daughter would find happiness in her marriage.

Before she knew it, she too was packing once more to head to court. Joan had suddenly remembered the Queen Dowager, who had died last February. The country mourned the loss of her stabling influence on her stepson, the king. She had been mistreated by him, for he gave her dower lands to Gaveston and exiled her for a while after she had supported his downfall. Yet she still loved and respected him.

She had been a saintly woman, and Joan wished to pay her homage. Since they were going to be in London anyway, she did not see how Roger could object.

~

London was a dreary sight when they rode through the gates. A fog covered the city and there was a sense of dreariness Joan could not help but notice. The people, it seemed, were unhappy and sensed that there would be more unrest in the kingdom, as Edward was once again showering his favorites with gifts he had no right to give, not to mention the fact that his coffers could not support such extravagances. It was well known that Edward took from others unjustly to give to his friends. It was making him very unpopular and in turn, seeing the hatred of his people, Edward began hating them too.

This whole business is a mess, Joan thought to herself and wished to be gone from the capital.

She was given rooms with Roger befitting their rank, and they dined with the king and his court every night. Gifts were handed out and there was much merrymaking after the somber masses of Easter.

Roger had been placated by a purse of one hundred gold marks that he had received as thanks for his efforts in Ireland. The wine and rich food he ate also helped to lull him into a resignation that Joan almost would have called affection for his king.

They were now at a mask. Joan was speaking to other ladies of the court to catch up on gossip. She had caught sight of the young Prince Edward, who unlike his father was blonde and carried himself with great pomp. Isabella kept him by her side, coddling him as any mother would, but at the same time she was keeping him away from his father's influence.

Joan learned it was no great secret that the beautiful Isabella detested her husband and there was great animosity between them.

She envied the queen's striking beauty and even grew to hate her when she noted how Roger's eyes followed her as she danced with her ladies-in-waiting.

Joan could say nothing to her husband, for she knew he was loyal enough. If he had strayed from their marriage bed, she did not know of it and, of course, she was no longer as beautiful as she once was. Her hair was now littered with streaks of gray that Joan thought were premature, and her skin was beginning to show its age as wrinkles began appearing where none had been before.

Being surrounded by the beautiful women of court made her notice these changes, and she sent a maid to procure face creams for herself and some dye to try to cover the gray.

Jane, who had only been married to Edwin for a couple of years, laughed at her mistress's sudden vanity but helped her nonetheless.

"When you are my age you will understand." Joan reassured her of this. "When your husband no longer comes to you at night, you will start to feel your age and resent these younger women."

Jane was twenty-six and she had yet to bear any children so had not lost any of her figure. Her husband did not complain but seemed to worship her.

"I would be pleased to have a chance to rest," Jane assured her longtime mistress, who only shook her head and stated simply that she would miss the ardent love when it had simmered down.

Still, Joan never questioned her position. She was the fertile Baroness Mortimer and perhaps one day, if her husband became an earl, then she would be a countess. No one could take her place.

~

They traveled around their lands visiting their many great houses before they went to Ludlow the following week. Joan wished to spend more time with her ailing mother. Roger moved on to Wigmore Castle, claiming to have business there.

Jeanne had an episode and the doctors who had managed to revive her said that they would not likely be able to do so again.

JOAN

Joan listened to this with a grieved heart. She had an interesting relationship with her mother and loved her despite the fact she received little love in return.

"I shall appoint a bailiff to help you and find a steward to manage this place fully. I don't want you to do anything but rest now," Joan ordered.

Jeanne rolled her eyes, but she had little fight left in her now.

Besides, at the ripe age of sixty she was overdue to retire from her duties.

Gathering the servants around Ludlow, Joan explained to them that her mother was not to be overtaxed or stressed in any way. Her heart would not be able to manage it. Many of the servants had served her a long time and were more than happy to comply, but Joan knew she would have to check on her mother as much as possible.

The next day she set out with a small guard and rode to Wigmore Castle. She still had her own duties and children to attend to.

When she arrived, the servants were extremely deferent but refused to meet her gaze. Joan thought nothing of this at first, but eventually she asked Jane to find out what was going on.

Jane returned to her with naught but a shrug. "They told me nothing."

Roger, who was out hunting, had not been any help either. Instead, he had been mad that she was so suspicious all of a sudden. So she decided to lay the matter to rest.

She had to visit her daughter Margaret, who was now pregnant with her first child and had little time to think of the whims of her servants.

Joan was pleasantly surprised to find her daughter so happy in her manor home and spent several days in her company.

It made her think of Edmund, who had been married but had yet to take up his duties as a husband since his bride was still too young. Soon it would be time for him to stop running around other ladies and give her a grandchild too.

No doubt he would be just as happy as Margaret seemed to be.

She went in search of Roger that summer day but could not find him in his offices or in the stables. As she wandered the castle, she thought of nothing but telling him of little Maggie.

It was then she heard hushed whispers and soft moans coming from the pantry. She was confused but thought of how she had discovered Simon in the arms of a serving wench. Frowning and ready to scold the perpetrators, she flung the door open.

What she saw nearly made her faint.

She rushed back to her rooms, ignoring her husband's calls.

In her room, she locked herself in and tried to calm herself, but tears came streaming down her face regardless and she let out great choking sobs.

She found her heart pounding hard in her chest and had to sit down to steady herself. After the shock passed and the tears stopped, rage and jealousy coiled in her heart like twin snakes.

She gave a little nervous laugh.

It was all right. It was to be expected; she was thirty-four. Her husband had not come to her bed since Easter. What did she expect?

Loyalty and love. That's what she expected.

She thought of all his sweet words and promises. The little gifts he had given her. They seemed so empty now.

Joan remembered how in the early days of her marriage she had kept a cool head and had not believed him.

Back then she had not loved him as she had come to now.

She was in so much pain she hardly knew what she should

do. Why did Roger have to betray her like this? Of course, this must have been going on for a while. The rest of the servants must have known, she thought, suddenly remembering their strange behavior. At least they did not seem to approve.

Gulping down some water, Joan realized by the darkened sky how late it was now.

Had she really been here for so long? She called for Jane to come to her.

She came as she was bidden, and when Joan told her of what she had seen she was understandably mortified. Jane had not heard an inkling.

"What will you do?" she inquired.

"Nothing, of course. I have confided my anger to you, but I must put this aside. There is nothing for me to do expect admonish my lord in private and pray that God forgives him for his sins." Joan touched her forehead and felt how hot she was. "Life must go on."

She tried to gather her strength about her but found she could not muster herself to go down to dinner.

When Jane returned that evening, she found Joan in bed with a fever and called for a physician.

She worried over her mistress, but the doctor assured her that this would pass. She had just been overtaxed.

The next day when Joan awoke she found Roger sitting in a chair by her side.

She blinked in surprise but said nothing, waiting for him to speak instead.

"I have sent her away." He shrugged at last. "I did not wish to make you so ill. I am a weak man."

She blinked again. Was that all he had to say?

At her silence, his own anger rose to the surface. "You should not have been searching around the castle like that. In any case, you know how it is between us. You are the mother of my children and I love you."

Joan knew that she would have to steel herself to accept this of him. She remembered how impetuous he was when he was a teenager and saw that if she pushed him away now, he would grow to hate her. She also realized that while he felt guilty for hurting her, he did not regret his actions.

Finally she spoke. "I had a fever. I am sorry to have worried you. I am your loyal and loving wife." She reached out her hand to him, which he grasped.

"All I ask is that if you do love another, please do not let me hear of it. For I could not bear it."

At her soft words, his eyes softened. She had struck a chord deep inside of him and he kissed her hand.

"I have no love but you. I promise to ever be your faithful knight."

She grinned at that, even though she knew they were empty words from an empty man. He knew nothing except fulfilling his own selfish desires. She had forgotten this but had remembered in her feverish dreams.

"When I am better perhaps I will visit my mother," she said to him, as though she was looking for permission.

"I will come with you," he promised. Kissing her hand again, he stood. "Get some rest."

With that, she was alone again.

She thought of her mother and father. Would she and Roger become like that? Living separate lives? But her mother had been content. She had never loved Piers de Geneville, not like she loved Roger.

CHAPTER 10

1321-1322

Roger had kept his promise to Joan and accompanied her to Ludlow, where they spent a week together. He visited her often during that time, and she fell pregnant with what she suspected were twins.

Joan had never recovered her trust in him nor loved him blindly as she used to. But Roger was none the wiser and she kept her feelings to herself.

Her mother's condition was worsening. Jeanne was now confined to bed fully or when she could manage it to a chair that servants carried to the garden or great hall. She reminded Joan of her grandfather, who had died in 1314 bedridden with his pains. She prayed her mother would improve or at least not suffer as much as he had in his last days.

Then, as she was tending to her, she received news that terrified her.

Roger's northern land had been given away to the Despensers, and Roger had called upon his kinsmen and other Marcher Lords to meet with him.

Joan had no doubt they talked of rebellion. With urgency, she left her mother's side and rushed back to Wigmore.

Of course, she was too late.

Roger and others had begun raiding the Despenser lands. Then Hugh de Bohun, Earl of Hereford, outright refused the king's summons.

The world was going mad and no one would listen to her.

Joan urged Roger for the sake of their children, who would lose everything if he was declared a traitor, to not act rashly.

Following this conversation, he had done just the opposite.

Joan's pregnancy prevented her from riding out or doing much more than sitting in bed when she heard that her husband, who she now assumed was insane, had ridden out, gathering men and hiring mercenaries to march upon London.

Days later Jane brought her news that the city had closed its gates to her husband, but instead of turning back he laid siege to the city.

At this news, Joan had the decency to faint.

The Despenser War was in full swing.

~

Joan cursed as the midwives told her to push.

But she was not cursing them or the babes about to be born. She was cursing her husband.

By some stroke of luck, with the help of Lancaster and Hereford he had been able to capture several of the Dispensers' lands, including Newport and Cardiff. There were others, but they slipped her mind as more and more grave news had poured in.

It was evident now that Roger's actions could not be seen as anything but treasonous, and she feared for herself and her children. She had given up hope for Roger.

Still, her husband's faction had seen several victories. Even Queen Isabella had pleaded that the king should listen to them and exile the Despensers, who were the source of all of these problems.

He had listened and the situation was defused for a time.

But now there was to be war and fighting again.

Roger was not with her now. She was huddled away at Ludlow, trying to be obscure as possible. She would have gone to Ireland in exile with her children if she felt there was a safe ship to take her.

Her mother was furious with Roger, and her anger gave her strength she had not had in a while. Jeanne berated Joan, who could do nothing to stop her husband. In fact, she had not seen or heard anything from him in a month. The news she heard was gossip and she did not know if she could trust it.

Finally, after three days of laboring her twins were born. It was another pair of girls. They were healthy enough, but Joan could barely find herself paying them much attention.

Peasants had risen up in revolt, and Roger and his uncle had to stifle it before joining Lancaster again. Joan was uneasy. She knew this was the chance the king would need to gather his army and march upon the rebels. She knew that after his siege of Leeds Castle he had regained some of his popularity with the people.

She drank heavily from her wine and was content to wait for news rather than worry about what could have been and what was.

They waited for many days in a self-imposed imprisonment.

Her younger children did not know what was going on but sensed something bad was happening, for they did not cry and throw tantrums as they used to do. Everyone was tense from waiting so long.

A man knocked at the side entrance of Ludlow. After explaining who he was to the gatekeeper, he was brought before Joan.

She vaguely recognized him as a man who served under her husband and hurried to his side.

"What is the news?"

"Surrender," he panted, still out of breath, for he had run here after his horse had fallen lame. "At Shrewsbury. Baron Mortimer and Master Roger de Chirk have been sent to the tower."

"Are they unharmed?" she asked, having already guessed they had lost.

"Yes, my lady. I ran away and came to tell you. I will run away to Scotland or France, lest they find and arrest me too."

"Master William. I remember you now!" Joan finally recognized him in the light of the fire.

He bowed. "I am sorry to bring you such terrible news."

Joan shook her head. "Thank you for bringing it. You did not have to." She snapped her fingers and a manservant appeared. "Fetch me a purse of silver for this man and make sure he has a sack of food for his journey."

She turned back to him. "I have no horse to give you, but I am sure you will make do."

He thanked her deeply, accepting her gracious gifts. It was more than he could have hoped for.

Joan rushed upstairs to her solar. She sat at her writing desk and wondered what and to whom she would write, imploring forgiveness for her husband.

In the end, she wrote two letters. One was to the king asking for a pardon for her husband, saying that she was still a loyal subject, and the other was to Queen Isabella to see if she would intercede on her husband's behalf as she had once done before.

JOAN

The weeks that followed were filled with fear for the whole household. As of yet, there was no news. It seemed that the king, who had now been victorious over Lancaster, was content with getting his revenge. He neither had Roger executed nor did he free him. Joan was left unmolested, though it was well known how far her family had fallen and they were seen as traitors now.

Eventually, business returned to normal and she went about seeing the house was kept right and that the serfs were working their hardest. No one mentioned their absent lord or the fact there were hardly any merchant visitors and even fewer noble ones. Then a letter came from her husband imploring her to visit him, for he was miserable and kept in terrible conditions.

Against her mother's advice, she packed a small saddlebag with money and a change of clothes for herself. Inside her riding cloak she had sewn her best jewel that she would give to Roger. It was the brooch of a prancing lion holding a sapphire surrounded by small diamonds. Roger had given it to her upon the birth of his son Edmund. She had treasured it but knew that he would have more use for it now. Perhaps he could buy himself favor with the guards and receive food and a warm fire.

With that happy thought, she jumped on the back of Marigold and rode off, with only Edwin to act as guard and guide.

When Joan arrived at the tower she balked at the heads displayed on spikes. Had she been a weaker woman she would have been sick at the sight. Instead, she walked up to the gates with a clear head.

There had been many words exchanged between her and the constable of the tower.

The man was not in the mood to let Roger Mortimer have visitors. But it had been several months since his imprisonment and the king had not given him any further instructions. He had not specifically said he could not have visitors. Seeing his grieved wife, the constable softened and said she could see him, but only for a couple of hours.

"And you may not bring anything in with you."

In an act of submission, Joan kneeled before him and kissed his hand in gratitude as she slipped him a gold coin.

She hated to beg, but she knew when to give thanks.

After waiting for a while, she was led up the steps to her husband. Roger leaped to his feet when he heard the guards approaching. No doubt he feared that he was to be executed now.

Joan almost laughed when she saw the expression on his face when he saw her enter. He had never looked so elated to see her face.

The guard locked the door after she entered and left them to speak in private.

"Husband, you are much changed." She noted his grizzled look and how thin he was. The room was also cold.

A freshly made fire was burning in the fireplace, but it had yet to warm the room. Joan looked at him with pity, for his letter was no lie: he was kept in dismal conditions. Though what could he expect?

"I—your children miss you and pray for you every day," she stammered.

"I am glad you have come to see me." He approached with naught but love in his eyes. A love that Joan instantly distrusted.

"I was worried when I received your letter," Joan murmured. "I could not let you suffer." She paused, holding his cold hands in hers. "I have paid for a warm supper to be sent to you."

Roger nodded in thanks then looked away as if in shame.

He had fallen so low that his wife needed to bribe his guards to bring him food.

"Your children are well but frightened. I am afraid we are pariahs now. No one wishes to know our family." She shook her head sadly.

"I did what had to be done. We had rotten luck, yet still I regret nothing. Those Despensers are evil!" Though he whispered this, his words seemed to echo throughout the room and Joan hushed him.

"There isn't much I can do for you. But I can leave you my cloak. You may find it a useful treasure." Without a word, lest someone was listening, she unclasped it from her neck and showed him where she had stitched the jewel.

When he saw it, he kissed her on the lips. "Bless you. This will be of great help."

Joan blushed, looking away. At this moment, she was her husband's most precious person of all, but she knew that the moment he was free he would turn away from her again. Already there were rumors that Queen Isabella had knelt before her husband to exile the Despensers for the love of Roger Mortimer. Joan had ignored these silly rumors, for she knew the queen hated the Despensers as well, and though her husband was still handsome, the queen would never stoop so low.

"I will try to plead your case to the king, not only for yourself but for our children also. You have not even met Maud and Blanche." Joan pulled away from him.

They spoke together by the fire, making plans for what should be done with the estates and how everything should be run in his absence. They did not mention the possibility of his death.

When the guard came to escort her outside, she held him tight one last time and made him promise he would keep himself safe.

Joan stayed with Edwin at an inn, not wishing to go to court and see if she would be allowed inside.

The next day she returned home to wait upon the king's pleasure, having sent him another letter pleading her case.

He had yet to send any reply, and Joan all but gave up hope. Still, she had received another letter from Roger saying he was well and thanking her for being such a steadfast wife.

～

That Christmas there was no celebration. Not only was Joan trying to save every penny she had, but she could not bring herself to be joyous.

She sent her serfs and tenants small gifts but did little else to acknowledge the season.

Time passed slowly for her and the children. They stayed around the castle and grounds. There were no talks of marriages or festivals. The only break they had from the monotony was attending mass at the local church.

The house was even more solemn when on a sunny spring day in April of 1323 Jeanne passed away from another episode with her heart.

Jeanne was sixty-three years old and had lived a long, full life.

Joan only despaired that her last few years were filled with such uncertainty and fear.

She wondered if she should be jealous of her mother for escaping this life of turmoil. For it seemed she faced nothing now but more pain and injustice.

The king's guards appeared at Ludlow at the end of August with an order from the king.

She was to go to Hampshire, one of her lesser houses, to be placed under house arrest.

They had packed away her daughters to be cared for in

religious houses around the country. Joan was horrified and begged the commander to tell her the reason.

He sneered at her and asked if she did not know that her husband had escaped jail and run away to France. Seeing her shock, for she had not heard even a whisper in these last few days, he decided to press the point home. Not only did Roger run away to France without a word to her, but he had also taken up with Queen Isabella in an adulterous relationship that would damn his soul.

Joan fainted at his words and had to be carried in a litter on the journey to Hampshire.

There was nothing left of her heart now. No consolation for her.

Her husband had bribed the guard to escape to France, where he bedded the English queen. He had not warned her nor seemed to care what became of his children.

Joan could not believe it had come to this.

All those years together meant nothing to him in the face of his ambition for power.

But she should have known. He was an empty faithless man.

∽

She faced endless hungry days and nights locked up in her rooms. She prayed that her children received better care.

They had been taken away from her, and she didn't know where they were. Joan's heart was breaking for the loss of them. They were all she had left in this world.

Cruelly, her guards gave her no news of the children. So she sent out a prayer every night, hoping that God was watching over them wherever they slept that night.

Her only visitors were a priest that came to hear her

confession once a week and a maid that cleaned the room but did not talk to her.

It was a piteous existence.

But slowly she found her courage and will to survive.

The king would forgive her eventually. He had to see she had been wronged just as he had been with a faithless spouse.

She would keep fighting for her family and for herself.

EPILOGUE

Agnes and Joan ran hand in hand to their mother. The twins had heard happy news and wished to be the first to tell her.

They did not knock on her bedroom door but barged in.

"What is the meaning of this, ladies?" Joan scolded them. They were guests at Pontefract Castle now, having been moved from Hampshire to Skipton Castle and then finally here. At Pontefract, the king had graciously sent all six of her youngest daughters to be with her. It seemed his anger toward her had dulled.

"I heard the servants talking—"

Agnes interrupted her sister. "They said Father had landed in England with the queen and her son—"

"And something about Lancaster capturing King Edward," Joan finished.

Their mother was unnerved by the way they finished each other's sentences but gasped when she understood the meaning.

Sure enough, a man appeared at her door confirming what her daughters had said. Unable to believe the news, Joan stayed a week longer at Pontefract then made plans to return to Ludlow and then Wigmore Castle.

She hesitated to write to Roger, who she detested for all the suffering she had gone through because of him. She had been mistreated on his account and imprisoned to punish him. Joan could have laughed at that. Did they not know that he did not love her? He would not care what happened to her.

∼

Finally, a month after she had been reunited with all her children at Wigmore, her eldest daughter Margaret, who was now a mother to three boys living happily in Gloucestershire, paid her a visit. Even she had been imprisoned temporarily until her husband vouched for her.

Katherine had turned twelve and was now nearing the age of adulthood. Joan had no doubt that she would soon join her husband, the Earl of Warwick, at his castle where they would hopefully lead a very prosperous life.

Sir Edmund, her heir and eldest son, had been imprisoned in the Tower of London with her other sons. He had been released by his triumphant father but had returned to her as a dutiful son. She did not wish to keep him long, for she knew he longed to be at court, where his father now ruled supreme with Queen Isabella.

Her son would soon be a father, and she clutched him in a tight hug at the news. Edmund boasted that his wife was so big she had to be carrying a son.

Eventually, one by one her eldest children departed to go home to their own estates and affairs. The country was abuzz with gossip about her husband and how he had killed King Edward II to put his younger son on the throne, how he now ruled as regent beside the queen. He was acting as de facto ruler of England—the pinnacle of his ambitions.

JOAN

Then she discovered he had been made Earl of March and had been given great lands and treasures.

She could no longer be content with being forgotten. Living like an invisible woman.

Now Joan could no longer pretend she was not married to Roger Mortimer. No matter her misgivings, she put aside her pride and wrote to him demanding as his wife that he see to their children's futures. She demanded nothing for herself, though in honesty she should have had a greater allowance. Instead, she lived as if she was already widowed, taking her percentage of the profits from the lands she had inherited.

She swore she would never see Roger again, and in truth she never did. He never replied nor wrote to her, but he did as she bid him.

She knew this business of his was folly and likely to crumble around him.

He reached too high. Like Icarus, who had flown too close to the sun and fell to his death as a result, Roger too would perish for his folly.

AUTHOR'S NOTE

As a disclaimer, I wish to state that this is a work of fiction and certain events and dates have been fabricated or may be based on incorrect information. I tried to stay true to the events of Joan de Geneville's life. As a result of her husband actions she had been imprisoned twice in her lifetime and we know she was not kept in the greatest of conditions. She had twelve children with Roger which makes me think that at first their marriage had been a happy one.

Undoubtedly, something deteriorated between them because Roger Mortimer did have an affair with Queen Isabella.

In 1330, Roger Mortimer was overthrown, imprisoned and finally hanged as a traitor at Tyburn, by King Edward III. The King eventually pardoned his wife, Joan and children who had once again been imprisoned on his account.

Sir Edmund Mortimer never inherited his father's lands however, his son Roger eventually regained the title of his grandfather becoming the 2nd Earl of March.

Joan had still been alive to witness her grandson inherit

AUTHOR'S NOTE

the titles that had rightfully belonged to him. She died at the age of seventy and was buried beside her husband.

Upon her death, her grandson Roger inherited Ludlow and many of her other estates.

Joan's story or lack thereof fascinated me. Who was the wife of the notorious traitor? What had she been like? And what had she thought of her husband's exploits?

While we may hear a lot about the life of Roger Mortimer we hear little of his wife.

In this story, I tried to tell her story as I imagined her: a flawed but powerful woman who managed to survive in tumultuous times.

This was the first installment of my series titled "Forgotten Women of History".

FORTUNA'S QUEEN

PROLOGUE: FORTUNA'S QUEEN

Pella, 356 BC

She was the daughter of the king of Epirus.

Yet here she was on her knees before Phillip of Macedonia, her husband.

She was rumored to have descended from the great Achilles himself, and if the rumors were accurate she had enough magic in her thumb to squash an empire. She wished that were true.

"Don't go." Her voice barely a whisper.

She kept her eyes to the ground as he stepped off his dais and approached her. She couldn't help but stiffen when he touched her bare shoulder with his hand.

"We all must do what is necessary for the kingdom." He lifted her off the ground and placed a kiss on her cold lips. "My beautiful wife, you must stay here and guard the kingdom and yourself." He placed a hand over her protruding belly.

"Take me with you then." She did not relent, even as she saw his eyes narrow in frustration and anger.

She was not some complacent cow to be left at home.

PROLOGUE: FORTUNA'S QUEEN

"Olympias." He chided her like her father used to when she was a little girl. "You should go rest."

She pulled out of his arms and stormed out of the hall in a flourish of gold and white linen.

The courtiers parted to let her through. They watched as this untouchable lady who commanded their respect brushed away the servants who moved forward to help her. Damn her husband, she cursed in her head as she marched down the halls and corridors.

It was only in her rooms among her loyal servants and her pets that her icy mask cracked and her fury reared its head.

She flung a vial of perfume, smiling satisfied when it hit the opposite wall and shattered, filling the air with the sweet smell of narcissus.

"Leave it," she hissed at a servant who bent to clean up the shards. "Leave, all of you." She dismissed her servants with a wave of her hand.

Olympias was well known for her fits of anger, and they left without another word. Ever since she had become pregnant these fits had increased in frequency. All the astrologers predicted that she was carrying a great warrior in her belly.

Olympias sat down on her couch piled high with silk cushions as she tried to calm herself.

The baby was kicking now.

"Warrior, indeed," she murmured as she caressed her belly, urging the child to calm down.

Phillip seemed determined to leave her behind as he went off to conquer new lands and expand his kingdom. She knew it was likely that she would be usurped from her position as his principal wife while he was away. Lords and kings alike would push forward their daughters, sisters, and nieces, hoping to catch the lustful king's eye. However, this was not the greatest danger she had sensed. She feared there would be a rift between father and son that could never be mended.

PROLOGUE: FORTUNA'S QUEEN

So bending the knee, she hoped she might prevail upon him to put off his campaigning for another month—no more. It was foolish to ask this, but for her son she would do anything. She would see him come to his throne, but for the moment his future was clouded and Olympias was scared what this meant.

She was also filled with anxiety that while Phillip was away from her Attalus would whisper in his ear until he finally convinced her husband she was a witch and that her son was not worthy to be his heir.

Phillip had another son by one of his inconsequential wives, but the child was slow and Phillip was eager to have a healthy replacement. It had been rumored that the child who had been born to a great destiny had been cursed by his nursemaid, who had been caught weaving a magical spell over him on the night of his first birthday.

One thing Phillip feared more than dying of old age was magic.

Olympias rolled her eyes at his fears and pitied the nursemaid, who had died a terrible death for doing nothing more than singing to her young charge a lullaby in her native tongue.

Such simple actions could be misinterpreted so easily, and the courtiers who were always searching for scandal had pounced on the opportunity to make trouble.

That had been nearly two years ago, when Olympias had arrived at the palace a fresh-faced youth. She had learned quickly to guard her secrets and do what she had to do to gain power in her own right.

As Phillip's wife, there was always a crowd of men and women dogging her steps, asking her to intercede with her husband on their behalf. Over the years, she had gained a loyal following and they protected her from the likes of Attalus. He was one of Phillip's most trusted commanders, who had high ambitions of connecting himself to the Argead dynasty through marriage. Attalus had plenty of pretty nieces, and Phillip's eyes were always wandering.

Luckily, Attalus was busy now with thoughts of war, but he was sure to return to his scheming the minute the fighting stopped. She frowned, wishing the gods would take his life in battle so she could be rid of him, but she had already scried his future and saw that death was not imminent for her rival.

She had to content herself with the fact that she would remain in Pella as Phillip's representative watching over his house. She would be alone to create further alliances and gain more power while both men were away.

Still, it was with a heavy heart that she watched Phillip depart at the head of his army.

He was a warrior through and through. He was not like other commanders who hung back while their soldiers fought their battles for them. This was the one thing she admired about him.

She watched him now standing in front of the altar holding the large sacrificial dagger near the bull's head as the priest finished intoning the last of the prayer to Ares to bring victory to the Macedonian army.

Olympias felt her heart soar with anticipation as she watched his strong arms swing upward, slicing through the bull's throat as though it was merely butter. She was mesmerized by the blood spurting from the wound as the bull bellowed one last time. It coated the steps of the temple even as the acolytes ran forward with a golden bowl to collect the draining blood.

"Victory!" the head priest called out after consulting the bowl, and a great cheer came from the gathered crowd and soldiers.

This was not to be the last of the sacrifices, but it was the most important. Hundreds of beasts were offered up to the gods to provide a speedy victory.

PROLOGUE: FORTUNA'S QUEEN

Phillip was confident that the Pheraeans and Phocians would be defeated swiftly, but he also prayed for a battle worthy of being remembered. He dreamed of glory as all men did and thought of expanding his kingdom. The Thessalian League had approached him last year asking for his help to get rid of the dictator Lycophran, who had managed to anger most of the ancient noble families of Thessaly. They wished to return to the old ways when they could manage their own affairs.

Phillip had jumped at the chance to involve himself in the politics of the region. He secretly dreamed of uniting all the Greek city-states under his name. He would rule all of Greece and then he would turn his attention to his dangerous neighbor to the east. The Persians were a constant threat and he dreamed of one day conquering them, but Macedonia could not do it alone.

∽

Perae, 355 BC

War had dragged on for longer than he had hoped.

He had been on campaign for over two years, and they were finally making steady progress. Ever since the Pheraeans had sacked the Temple of Delphi, his army had been invigorated with a new cause. Now they fought to overthrow the sacrilegious Pheraeans and defend Apollo's honor.

At his side, Nicesipolis stirred, murmuring something in her sleep. Phillip frowned and wrapped his arms around his newest wife to protect her from her evil dreams. In his embrace, she stilled once more and he kissed her brow.

Back in Pella, his newest son Alexander was getting stronger with each passing day. He had been born with a crown of blond hair like his mother's. The child had too much

PROLOGUE: FORTUNA'S QUEEN

of Olympias in him, and he found himself already resenting the growing boy.

Phillip believed that he was jealous of the love Olympias gave to Alexander. He wanted her to feel the same toward him. In their first years of marriage, he had doted on her and came to love her with a fervor that terrified him at times.

He even put up with the snakes Olympias insisted on keeping, despite the rumors of witchcraft that his courtiers liked to whisper in his ears knowing how terrified he was of evil magic. Desiring her love and admiration, he ignored them, but still he did not receive what he wanted from her.

Instead, she seemed content to threaten him with the gods' wrath if he displeased her.

He worshiped the gods but also trembled at their power.

They had razed cities like Troy to the ground and snuffed the light out of greater men than him.

He had come to his throne by right and ruled with a sword in his hand. He had molded Macedonia from a backwater province into the great kingdom it was today. But in a moment, all of his work could be washed away on the whim of an immortal who cared nothing for the blood and sweat he had poured into his land.

So Phillip harbored a fear of them that he could not get rid of. People liked to claim that he was blessed by the gods, but Phillip would rather he remain anonymous. It was safer than drawing their attention.

Nicesipolis shifted and her hand rested on his chest as though she wanted to comfort and wash away his dark thoughts. It was she who had suggested mildly that he was Apollo's champion.

On his behalf, he should destroy those who had sacked his temple. If he did this, Apollo would see his enemies driven into the sea.

His normally gentle wife had surprised him with her

PROLOGUE: FORTUNA'S QUEEN

vicious sentiments. Just as soon as she had finished speaking, her usually innocent countenance had returned.

He wondered if she had been touched by a divine vision or influenced by Apollo himself.

The thought had led him to seriously consider his next actions. After conferring with his commanders, he had come up with the perfect plan. His men would go out to battle wearing crowns of laurels for Apollo—they would be his soldiers.

Perhaps Apollo would grant them the victory for the honor they bestowed on him.

It was also a shrewd political move. The Pheraeans and their allies would think twice about continuing to fight against him. Their morale would surely be lost in the face of the righteous wrath of the Macedonian army.

But now his thoughts turned away from war as he regarded his dark-haired Thessalian wife.

She was everything Olympias was not. She might not have been as nobly born, but where Olympias was sharp, she was soft. Where Olympias was war, she was peace.

Phillip ran his hands through Nicesipolis's dark curls. She was an innocent youth, seemingly untouched by ambition or hatred. She loved him with those dark eyes of hers and seemed to melt in his arms.

For his part, he adored her devotion to him. His courtiers and politicians had been surprised when he had declared he would marry her.

They thought perhaps she would be another of his concubines, but he had honored her with a proper marriage. Any children she had would be legitimate heirs. This thought pleased him.

He thought of Alexander again. The last time he had seen him he had kicked at his father and regarded him with a cool hatred when Phillip pulled his mother away to his rooms. Such anger did not belong on a child's face. Did Olympias plot against him and poison his son's mind against him? She was about to give birth again, and he feared that it would be another son, another rival for his throne.

Any children he had with Nicesipolis would surely adore and honor him. Before he allowed himself to fall into a deep sleep, he made a note to call the astrologer tomorrow to read her charts, and after that he would put his soldiers through their paces.

∽

Pella, 349 BC

Olympias drummed her nails on the table, irritated as she listened to the latest report from Thessaly.

The steward looked as though he was about to start quaking in his sandals.

Coiled around her left arm and resting contently on her shoulder blades was her black python, Kelainos. No doubt the steward thought she would have him fed to the snake if he displeased her.

Dressed in a robe as dark as her pet, with her hair piled high on her head and captured in a net of pearls, she looked every bit the sorceress. They were ridiculous, the rumors that sprang forth about her, but she used them to her advantage. Fear gave her control.

"Lydus, are you keeping something from me?" She petted the snake's head with her free hand.

"N-no. That is to say, the king has ordered jewels and silk to be sent to Thessaly. Nothing to trouble yourself over." He bowed low in an effort to hide his shaking.

"There's no need to be afraid. You have been a loyal servant, Lydus. Besides, Kelainos does not bite unless I ask him

PROLOGUE: FORTUNA'S QUEEN

to." Olympias gave a chilling laugh and dismissed the frightened man. She wondered if he would have fainted if she had tormented him a moment longer.

Once he was gone she snapped her fingers and her personal handmaidens stepped forward. Carefully, they helped her unwind her stubborn pet from her arm and put him back in his basket.

Her favored lady, Niobe, hung by her side waiting for instructions.

"Send him a small purse of silver for his honesty. I fear I may have gone too far with my antics tonight. After that please tell the cooks to be generous with the food and to bring out as much wine as my guests require tonight."

Niobe bowed her head and left to see to her tasks.

Now that she was left alone and without her snake draped over her, Olympias no longer looked like the powerful sorceress queen. She was merely a tired twenty-year-old woman, with two children to look after. She walked to their rooms and watched from afar as they played in the arms of servants.

Alexander was nearly three years old, big for his age, with curly hair like her own. Cleopatra was only two months old and, much to Olympias's dismay, seemed to favor her father's darker appearance, but she was a sweet quiet baby. There was a distinct difference between Cleopatra and Alexander, who even as a newborn had not given his nursemaid a moment's peace.

Lanike, Alexander's nursemaid, spotted her and when he was distracted with a toy walked over to her, bowing respectfully. "The children seem happy today. Cleopatra has just awoken from a nap if you would like to hold her."

Olympias shook her head. She did not have time to play with her children now, but tonight she would pull them into her arms and cradle them until they fell asleep. "Has Alexander been behaving?"

"He tried to escape from us twice, but I caught him."

"He will become unmanageable the more he grows." Olympias shook her head and then left the children to their games.

She was a fiercely protective mother. All the servants had been handpicked and interviewed by her personally. She kept the children close to her own rooms and guarded them against sickness and disease. Phillip wrote to her frequently warning her not to coddle their son. He needed to become a warrior, not a whimpering child hiding behind his mother's skirts.

Olympias was furious he would dare make such an accusation. She dreamed of great things for her golden-haired son, but for now he was too young to protect himself.

Back in her private rooms, her desk was now neatly organized. Scrolls and tablets were neatly arranged for her perusal. There was nothing there that she did not already know. The army needed a constant stream of food and supplies, which she oversaw with an easy proficiency. The rest were the requests of noblemen begging for favors, which could wait a few more days.

She fiddled with the gold band around her left arm. Was Nicesipolis a rival or a passing fancy? She had heard of Phillip's new marriage a few days after it had taken place. He had wanted to keep it quiet, no doubt fearing what she would think, but Olympias had merely shrugged. Phillip had never been faithful, nor did she expect him to be. He was a king and needed to gain favor and power through marriages and alliances.

But then rumors began that this woman who had barely any noble blood in her at all was constantly by his side. At night, she would whisper to him and they would retire before

PROLOGUE: FORTUNA'S QUEEN

Phillip had too much to drink and became rowdy. Whatever she wanted, he seemed more than happy to procure for her.

"Witchcraft" was whispered among the courtiers and servants at Pella. They had never seen this girl before, but they did not doubt that something was afoot.

Some approached Olympias warning her of this new wife and her magical powers.

"She controls the minds of men with the mere sound of her voice. With a touch, she could send a man to his grave," they whispered.

Olympias laughed and waved them aside. These were the same rumors she had heard about herself. In the past, Phillip had liked to taunt her with them. "My little witch," he had whispered into her silvery blond hair as he clutched her at night.

Then, out of resentment, she began to emulate the very thing he teased her with, and then he began to fear her as well.

To many she had indeed become a witch, but it was not through magic but rather deceit and wit that Olympias kept her enemies at bay. She played one faction against the other until she achieved the outcome she wished for and no one was the wiser. To her friends she was a generous benefactress, to her enemies she was a viper, but she always had to watch her back.

Phillip had begun to keep his distance as well. He did not believe she was a witch, but he was smart enough to know that she had just as deadly skills up her sleeves.

Between her snakes and poisons, he could not trust her, and now that she had a son who had a claim on his throne he was even more fearful, though he was loath to admit that he was afraid of a woman, much less his own wife.

"How the men would laugh if they saw their great ruler shaking before his wife." She remembered laughing at him when he had stumbled into her room one night drunk. He trembled when he saw her with a snake entangled around her middle.

He had backed away frightened, but at her words had stepped forward and rewarded her with a sharp slap. Still she had laughed, and he fled the room.

That had been the last time he had gone to her rooms in nearly a year.

Olympias sighed. Her bed remained cold, but she would not risk taking a lover. Any whiff of scandal would give Phillip the excuse to declare Alexander illegitimate and get rid of her too.

Now Phillip wanted to lavish his favorite with gifts and jewels when the kingdom's coffers were straining from war? Well, who was she to stop him?

—End of Preview—